THE
DISAPPEARANCE OF
ALEXANDER
SCHOBER

Crime Novel No. 1 ° English Edition

Veronika Bellone & Thomas Matla

THE DISAPPEARANCE OF ALEXANDER SCHOBER

Crime Novel No. 1 ° English Edition

THE SWISS FRANCHISE DETECTIVES

THE DISAPPEARANCE OF ALEXANDER SCHOBER
Book series: THE SWISS FRANCHISE DETECTIVES
Crime Novel No. 1 – English Edition
© 2024 Veronika Bellone & Thomas Matla
Kontakt@Kunstwirtschaftler.com
www.Kunstwirtschaftler.com

Production and publishing: BoD - Books on Demand, Norderstedt
ISBN (Print): 9 783 759 721 907

Preface

Loretta Lombardi, not averse to all things Italian and sensual, and Lars Van de Velde, an Amsterdam born cycling and Japan enthusiast, are the partners of the Swiss detective agency *Lombardi International Franchise Investigations AG*, in the city of Zug. Both detectives fight for the good in franchising on behalf of clients, track down black sheep and solve mysterious cases. More than once, they have to make use of their fighting skills. They are supported in their battle against the dark side of franchising by Regula Rhyser from Aargau, Carmen Cadruvi from Graubünden, Morita Miramoto from Japan and Sara Antić, who was born in Schwyz.

In this first volume of the franchise crime series Alexander Schober, the former owner of a family business, disappears without a trace in Ticino. His successor, newly active in franchising, calls in detective Loretta Lombardi to find him. Schober had previously landed an important coup. He has developed new recipes that are crucial for the expansion of the franchise. Loretta plunges into a sea of entanglements.

The Disappearance of Alexander Schober

1

"The hands are trying to hold on to the rock wall. To no avail. The feet slip away. Branches whip against the face. A small desperate stop. Free fall...loud crash."

2

"Shit!" Blood mixed with the puddle of water. The shards of glass were as sharp as carving knives. Loretta dug a handkerchief out of the bedside table where a glass of water had just been standing. With a makeshift thumb, she turned on the coffee machine.

"It's slowly getting enough. First this disgusting guy who tried to dump me. And now this horror in the dream. What's that supposed to mean? Hopefully this isn't prediction. And now I'm talking to the coffee machine too."

She opened the shutters and then there it was, the look that made up for everything. Blue sky, sun and a polished mountain panorama reflected in Lake Lucerne. From this distance, Lucerne looked like a lovingly designed toy town. A perfect spring day. Maybe something could come of the day after all.

3

"Buongiorno Signora Lombardi, would you like to try Sardinian pomodori? Freschi e sodi!"

"No grazie Luigi, today I just need fresh herbs," Loretta gestured with her hand to the opposite side of the market stall.

"Didn't you hear, Luigi, she doesn't want tomatoes or your dachshund look! That's four francs fifty, Mrs. Lombardi, and one franc for your thoughts," Elsie laughed harshly, as she had learned to do after almost thirty years of marriage to Luigi, and passed two lush bouquets of rosemary and thyme over the vegetable and herb displays.

"Elsie, you're lucky today! You rhymed," and Loretta murmured more to herself, "and honestly, you don't want to know my thoughts" because she wanted to forget them herself. Maybe a homemade herb quiche helped over the last, massively disturbing case.

Luigi still stood there grinning. However, his grin was less aimed at the fleshy, plump tomatoes in his hands than at Loretta's shapely figure, who appeared very sexy in a casual jeans and sweater outfit on this spring Saturday.

Actually, in her mood, she would have liked to hurl a sharp remark at him, but something loosened within her and she had to laugh. A liberating laugh. It was like someone clapped his hands and woke her up. Luigi, even at about fifty, with gapped teeth and a developing belly, was a daredevil and admirer of female charms. He may not have been the awakening that an attractive woman dreamed of, but he still had that Italian charm that simply couldn't be beaten and that had such an invigorating effect on Loretta.

"Oh, Mrs. Lombardi, I could use some luck. My sister lost her husband. So not actually lost - but she doesn't know where he is. He disappeared in Ticino."

Elsie's mood changed in a flash and she looked seriously at Loretta, who was still slightly amused putting the herbs at the top of the shopping basket, but then asked incredulously:

"Disappeared in Ticino?" Secretly she thought: "Well, that could easily happen to me too. Bella Ticino." She refused to suspect anything threatening at that moment: "The Italian part of Switzerland was known for its wildly romantic landscape, for its Romanesque churches and excellent cuisine, but not for atrocities," she thought.

"Yeah, I didn't even tell you that. They have a holiday home there. Luigi and I can use that from time to time. But we rarely have time."

"And money," Elsie thought, but then remembered what she actually wanted to say.

"Alex left on Wednesday and wanted to stay for the weekend. But there has been no sign of life from him since Wednesday evening. He's just gone! Disappeared without a trace!"

Elsie blew her nose excitedly with a wad of tissue paper, but quickly tried to get herself under control. There were still a few hours of work ahead of her. And although Luigi had returned to top sales form, his second spring made him unreliable.

Loretta handed Elsie a new handkerchief. She felt a little guilty for not showing concern.

"A kidnapping?" she asked quietly, because a woman next to her had apparently been looking for the ideal eggplant for a long time. Elsie shook her head and stared at a spot in the distance as if she recognized her brother-in-law there.

"Did he have problems? Withdrawal can sometimes be very healing. Loretta knew what she was talking about, privately she liked to withdraw when things got difficult. The complete opposite of her

11

professional alter ego. She only really felt at home when an order turned out to be particularly tricky and her strong combination skills were required.

"No, niente problemi," said Elsie firmly, always shedding her Swiss-German origins when Italian gave more pathos.

"How do you know that for sure? Have the police been called in?" Loretta had now completely switched to business mode.

"My sister is coming here from Zurich on Monday and will report what's new. If there's something new, hopefully." The eggplant woman still hadn't found what she was looking for, but was noticeably disappointed that the conversation seemed to be over. More customers had moved forward to her right and left and were slowly becoming impatient. Loretta pulled out her business card case, the most important item in the side pocket of her handbag alongside the handkerchief, lipstick and key ring, and handed Elsie a card.

She said goodbye with a warm-hearted: "Contact me if you need help. Ciao Elsie."

Elsie was a market woman again, catching all the customers with a look from her small, sparkling eyes, signaling that she was immediately there for them. Beforehand, she looked curiously at Loretta's card, which she held out at arm's length and read at the back of the stand. She let out an appreciative hiss that was probably meant to be a whistle, but failed due to the mixture of irritation and amazement.

Lombardi – International Franchise Investigations AG, Loretta Lombardi, partner, had stood there. She stowed the card in her voluminous jacket pocket, wisely in the inside pocket where it was most likely to stay wrinkle-free and clean. She still couldn't figure out what that meant exactly. In fact, she had always suspected that Loretta might have worked in the fashion or art industries based on her appearance and eloquence. Or an editor for a cooking magazine. At least something that had to do with joy and enjoyment of life. She was more familiar with her health insurance franchise. But what does this mean with this investment? Maybe investigators? But what is she investigating? Elsie stared after Loretta as if she was seeing her for the first time and not as if she was serving her at the weekly market for a good 10 years.

Loretta also knew that she had crossed a line. Mrs. Lombardi, with whom Elsie and Luigi had been able to exchange friendly words, discuss recipes and complain about the weather for years, had now mutated into the owner of a detective agency. The pleasant anonymity was gone. Elsie would now no longer interpret Loretta's lost thought, which she sometimes displayed, as a sleepy or dreamy peculiarity, but rather as the search for clues by an investigator who was currently following a lead in her parallel mental world.

"Hello Loretta, are you still working or are you already alive?" Fred Winter was amused as he strolled straight from the *Chapel Bridge* towards her. He stuffed the digital camera into the baggy pocket of his hoodie.

"And you, did you go among the tourists? 3,000 photos of Lucerne in the morning; 5,000 from the Ice Palace on the Jungfraujoch in the afternoon and Paris tomorrow? A trip around the world in twelve days?" countered Loretta quickly, as usual.

"It's nice to mingle with the people for once. Lucerne is simply unbelievably beautiful in this weather!" Fred was once again enthusiastic. And he was right. The sky was shining, the panorama was unique and the Reuss was almost turquoise due to the melting snow.

"And - *Mount Pilate* wears a hat!" he turned to Loretta and gave her a kiss on the cheek as if in confirmation.

"Yes, yes, Fred-Baby, then the weather will stay good!" Loretta looked at the cloud formation on the mountain top, which only barely resembled a head covering, but it was all about the saying. And if it was positive, even better.

"Come on, let's go to the Kranich and have an aperitif. And you tell me something bizarre about your life!" Fred had already linked arms with Loretta, taken over the shopping basket and was pulling her towards the Kornmarkt.

"Great, I come across as bizarre. Mid-forties, brunette, still pretty, feminine, quirky counterpart to Sherlock Holmes tells a story about her mysterious life. I have to rethink my image!" Loretta teased.

"Honey, you know that you're a sharp sweeper and that makes your brilliant mind a little more worldly." Fred had stopped, stood in front of her, smiling, the basket casually in the crook of his arm and measuring her exaggeratedly with his eyes.

"Well, how did I say that? I deserve a little wine for that."

"Are you all feeling spring today? Men!"

Loretta suddenly felt exhilarated. Compliments felt good. She was definitely a classy person and was in good shape for her age. And as if to confirm herself, she rushed up the stairs to the Kornmarkt, took the steps two at a time and then stood, quite out of breath but very much alive, on the historic square in the middle of the old town. Fred took it easy and sat down next to Loretta on one of those uncomfortable wooden chairs in front of the bar. But at least they had managed to get two seats in the sun, which was actually an impossibility at that time. Loretta had already ordered two glasses of Riesling, water and two portions of fish crispies.

Even though they weren't a couple, they knew each other's preferences in food, drink and more. And nicknames were common in their conversation. *Fred-Baby*, from Loretta's favorite film *Breakfast at Tiffany's*, was almost an award. The generic expressions: *darling* and *mouse* were used when Fred had to act as an extra again in order to make some situations during investigations more believable.

He never knew what it was all about, but he enjoyed being the supposed lover, co-worker, brother or whatever and thus taking on the role in a case. A welcome change and inspiration in his life as a comic artist.

Loretta was not only a long-time friend for him, but also the basis for a comic series in which she, as sexy researcher Brenda, discovered new planets and taught aliens to fear. The series was quite successful and was sold throughout German-speaking countries as well as in Japan.

Barbara, Fred's new girlfriend, found the familiarity between the two less exciting. As an architect, she was certainly a free spirit, but she sometimes gave free rein to her jealousy by providing him with scenes that were worthy of a film. Cups, pens or simply something quick to grab would fly around when words were no longer enough. He then let his inner camera run, retreated into his "money storage," as he called it, and creatively implemented the fresh images in his memory. That gave his comic characters this authenticity.

In analogy to Scrooge McDuck's money storage, he knew that it wasn't the bath in the money that gave him pleasure, but the scene of facial expressions and postures with which he earned a handsome fee. Loretta had just eaten the last of the fish crispy with a bit of tartar sauce and was apparently relaxed, squinting into the warm spring sun.

"Fred-Baby, have you ever not gone home? So, have you ever cut yourself off for a long time and left your girlfriend - what's her name - in the dark?"

Fred looked at her from the side, the striking profile with the boldly curved nose and the full lips, both of which indicated her Italian roots and had been immortalized in a somewhat more dramatized way than Brenda.

"B-A-R-B-A-R-A!" said Fred onomatopoeically, who now let his gaze wander over the busy square again.

"What do you mean exactly? Sure, I already stayed away. You should know that best. After all, I'm your extra often enough." Fred put on a broad smile.

"Yes, of course, that's not what I mean. But have you ever left without telling Barbara? Or did you want to?" Loretta had leaned back again, but didn't take her eyes off Fred so he had to answer.

"No, not really. It's kind of unfair when other people worry just because I can't get something sorted out!" Fred visibly enjoyed the last sip of wine and ordered two more ones. "One deci of wine is damn little. I see you feel the same way, Brenda."

Fred realized that Loretta was messing around with a case again. Whenever he noticed this change in her, he always called her Brenda.

"What are typical reasons?" Loretta, as Brenda, could now return to her questions straight away and looked at Fred challengingly.

"Another woman. There are these guys who lead double lives. Here a woman with a child, a house and all the bells and whistles and there a blueprint of it or a lover to whom he promises a great life. And at some point, he might no longer be able to bake the "Double Lottchen". I'm wondering how they manage it anyway. So financially, timely, mentally – yes and somehow also potentially. You know, potency-wise." Fred laughed at his own pun.

"Well the latter is probably the least of the problems! What else is possible besides this double life number? Fear, escape from something or someone?" Loretta was now in her element.

"To do this, of course, I need to know what social and business environment he operates in. Maybe they have financial problems. Well, if it gets too private, I'll have to hand over the case."

"Brenda, darling, don't you know anything about this man?" Fred had lost the thread a little, the moment was too beautiful. Sitting in the sun, a glass of wine on the table, pretty tourists passing by and his full-blooded girlfriend at his side - who just remembered a new Brenda episode. Life was so beautiful.

"Let's call it a day, Loretta. Monday is also another day. What's your Watson doing?"

"What does it mean *my Watson*? Let me remind you that not long ago you spent an entire night mixing cocktails that were meant to be somewhat cartoonish! *Captain Future Hurricane*! *Mr. Spock something* and finally this girl thing..." Loretta exclaimed.

"*The Lara Croft* cocktail is not a girl's thing, especially not at the end. It was also thematically appropriate for the *Fumetto Comic Festival*! Cult characters, great topic!" mused Fred and went into raptures.

"And if you opt out after dinner, the two of us just had to continue experimenting. Well, my head was a bit like *Moonhead* after that." He grabbed an imaginary head the size of a giant pumpkin.

"I think you weren't the only Moonhead. In any case, our Watson suffered quite a bit the next day." Loretta hadn't been happy with Fred encouraging him to start a long night. It had been a really nice day. Not for business. Three comic fans who tried to experience all the highlights of the festival in a few hours. Fred as a professional, she as an art enthusiast and Watson, alias Lars Van de Velde, co-owner of her detective agency for five years, both a brilliant profiler and a detective, a passionate cyclist and muesli eater, as a manga fan!

"Manga fan", Loretta had looked back over the images from the day and said the last thought quietly.

"I wouldn't have thought so. But I don't actually know him very well as a private person."

Fred looked at Loretta, who was talking more to herself than to him, and was surprised to feel a slight tug. It couldn't be jealousy, Loretta was like a good friend, a partner. He could discuss anything with her. They were close. Maybe that was it. Loretta was glad that her cell phone rang at that moment.

"Ha, you won't believe it! Speaking of the devil, he is sure to appear. Lars wrote. But all business."

4

"Grüezi miteinand!", Morita Miramoto, Lars Van de Velde's assistant, sat down at the table with a smile and enjoyed the look from those present, who always grinned at his Swiss-German greeting.

"Morita, have you seen Lars? Otherwise he is always punctual," said Regula Rhyser in astonishment.

"No, sorry, Legula." Regula suppressed a smile. Morita had that charming *L sound* for the letter *R*, which was otherwise subtle but more noticeable on Regula.

"I would like to start. There are urgent appointments on the agenda." She had just finished her sentence when Lars took his seat. He exuded fresh air from every pore.

"Sorry, but the new construction site is an obstacle even for cyclists," as he poured water into his oversized glass and drank it in one go. "Have you started yet?"

"No, but then we can start now. I have a very fitting task for you," Regula showed her famous You-made-my-Day smile.

"The *Big Tom* System, you know, this large bicycle chain with headquarters in Basel, has the problem that bicycles keep disappearing. There's not much more to say. Please clarify the details as quickly as possible, in order to stay in the mobility language. The thefts are probably increasing more and more." She included Morita, who was already giving Lars a thumbs-up sign.

"Sara will sent you Big Tom's contact details as well as some news about an insurance claim in Rheinfelden. Looks like exciting profiler work". Regula scrolled down her list of things to do and looked over at Loretta.

"And then we have another new case, the Schober AG in Niederbuchsiten, canton Solothurn. A Swiss master partner of a British fast food system called *Wings to heaven*."

"Wow! Awesome!" Carmen Cadruvi, Loretta's assistant, beamed from ear to ear. "My favorite brand."

"Fine, Carmen. Unfortunately, what is less nice is that the former owner and managing director Alexander Schober has disappeared. Loretta, I have already emailed you information about this and an appointment with the CEO of Schober AG for this afternoon agreed. Daniel Burmann, that's his name, is pretty nervous. A lot depends on this Mr. Schober. Carmen, you can do some research on your favorite brand."

Carmen uttered a heartfelt "Grazcha fich!" in Grisons, her Graubünden dialect, the language of her origins.

"Do you know since when Alexander Schober disappeared?" Loretta opened her *Moleskine*, which was also a sketchbook and a recipe book, and waited for Regula's answer.

"I'm not entirely sure, but I think it's been about five days. The police have been informed, but advise waiting. Because there is no evidence of a kidnapping or any other crime. Maybe he just disappeared. Mr. Burmann seems worried that he hasn't heard anything from Schober, firstly because he's supposed to be such a reliable person and secondly because Wings to heaven is currently in important expansion negotiations."

Regula took the last sip of her tea. A slightly honey-colored drink that was irritating due to the fluff floating in it. It had to be something healthy, Loretta thought. For some time now, Regula had stored a large selection of teas and powders in the office kitchen.

Loretta had gotten used to Lars' various green teas, but these strikingly designed health packs with the flavored scents were - to put it carefully - exhausting. Loretta fervently hoped that Regula would one day be healthy enough to indulge in real pleasure again. Just like everyone in the office knew her. Regula Rhyser was the soul of the detective agency. Correct, disciplined, completely reliable and endowed with a human warmth that led customers to call more often than the case required. There was something in her voice, in her manner, that made others want to confide in her, knowing that confidential matters were safe with her. This wasn't just the case with customers. She was also the focal point in the office when someone had a problem or a heartbreak, needed a sewing kit or a granola bar. Regula was the point of contact for everything. And she was secretive. Only something seemed to be moving her that morning. She was so different!

"Loretta. Can I speak to you briefly?" In addition to the digital information, Regula had placed a flyer about Wings to Heaven on Loretta's desk.

"Yes, of course, Regula." Loretta followed Regula with her eyes as she went to the door to close it.

"I got an offer. You probably remember Mr. Hegli from the Liquid Nutrition Concept. He called me all the time and showered me with his health packages, because he was so happy with the results that we, you and Carmen, found out."

25

Loretta took advantage of the slight pause in Regula's flow and asked impatiently. "And what does he want from you? Does he want to marry you? Or does he want you in his system?" Both felt terrible to Loretta. Regula was her closest confidant in the office and much more than that. She was simply indispensable.

"That's just the question. He offers me the management of coordination of franchise development and expansion. They are already internationally positioned, but they want to introduce a second brand and need someone who is strong in terms of projects but can also build bridges. It sounds appealing. But of course, I feel very comfortable here and I can hardly imagine leaving." Regula had sat down on the chair and was smoothing down the skirt of her costume. As she returned Loretta's gaze, she saw the range of emotions in her eyes and posture.

"Oops, that's really unexpected. Now I know what you mean by saying *The greatest step is that out of doors.*" Loretta took a sip of her now cold coffee. Actually, it was absurd for her, but she had to take a short break and find her attitude again.

"Of course I'm happy for you. Now it also explains why we have all these miracle teas and powders in the kitchen." Loretta had little experience in such conversations and tried to appear less affected with a little humor.

"It's a great offer for you. A new challenge. I can't imagine what it will be like here without you, but what does it look like? Have you checked it for yourself? What schedule are we talking about?"

"No, I haven't decided anything yet. I just wanted to let you know right away. We've known each other for so long and I think it's just fair. It would be at the beginning of the year, so next year, in January they see themselves in the starting phase. I'm not sure at all, Loretta. I also want to clarify what Michael is all about. I mean, Michael Hegli."

"Michael, how private are you?" Loretta looked at Regula a little confused.

"Oh, from my side, it's just a good understanding. We can talk about business well. I find the products exciting. Well, I have to think about it calmly. I'm sorry that I offended you like that." With that, Regula stood up straight and demonstrated that she had everything under control again.

"I have to go to Sara. She still needs some administrative support."

Loretta absentmindedly took the flyer in her hand and saw the photos with crispy chicken wings and the full-bodied quality statements when the telephone trumpeted - there was no other way to describe the new ringtone. The system technician had assigned ring tones for the various telephone lines according to his own wishes. His preference seemed to be general staff fanfare sounds.

"Mrs. Elsie Caruso would like to speak to you," Carmen rolled Caruso's *R* with her Graubünden dialect so wonderfully that Loretta had to smile.

"Thanks, please put her through."

"Buon Giorno, Mrs. Caruso, how are you? Is there anything new from your brother-in-law?"

"Buon Giorno, Mrs. Lombardi, I... I don't even know how to begin. My son looked at your website. I thought you were in the insurance industry because there was something about franchises on your card, but you're d-e-t-e-c-t-i-v-e." The way Elsie said it, she made the word sound like something mysterious.

"No, we only deal with insurance companies when we investigate something for them. But tell me if there's anything new. Depending on the situation, I can recommend a detective agency for private investigations."

28

"There are no clues, absolutely nothing. Not that anything happened to him either."

"Is he in good health?" As Loretta asked the question, she scribbled something hieroglyphic in her notebook that was next to the phone.

"Yes, very good. Luigi always says he's too thin and pale. He calls him *Porro* and because he's in the lab all day, he calls him *Professore Porro*," Elsie laughed briefly. "Luigi has vegetable names for everything and everyone. I am his *patate dolce*."

"That's lovely. Everything sounds much more charming in Italian anyway. Can you think of any reason why your brother-in-law, Mr. – what's his name exactly – disappeared?"

"His name is Alex, Alexander Schober."

"Wait, Alexander Schober, from Schober AG in Niederbuchsiten?"

"Yes, exactly. You know my brother-in-law?"

"No, I just read about the realignment of Schober AG in the newspaper."

"Yes, that's right. You are well informed. For Alex, it all happened much too quickly. Because he's such an inventor and has developed new sauces for it." Elsie paused. "Oh, Mrs. Lombardi, do you think you can help us find Alex?"

"Dear Mrs. Caruso, I thank you for your trust. As I told you, private investigations aren't normally my area of responsibility. But as luck would have it, I have business dealings with the Schober company. Information about Alexander Schober's personality and living conditions would be very useful to me. Do you think you and your sister can come and see me tomorrow morning? She wanted to visit you, right?"

"Yes, she's coming this afternoon. I'll set this up. Is there something bad with my brother-in-law's company? I mean, is there something wrong?"

"No, it's about expanding the company. But let's discuss this when you come over."

"Bernadette, my sister, always said that this company was making us all miserable."

5

"Carmen, can you come here please." Loretta had various files open on her screen. "It is written quite harshly here that the family business, Schober Saucen GmbH, will probably no longer see a fourth generation. Sales have fallen dramatically. According to Alexander Schober, it is due to the cheap goods from abroad. Convenience sauces and dips are flooding the entire market. Everything over-flavored with flavor enhancers. No quality standards."

"When was this published?" Carmen leaned over Loretta's shoulder.

"November 2017. But six months later the world looked different." Loretta opened an entry in Moneyhouse in which Daniel Burmann was named as CEO and majority shareholder of Schober AG, formerly Schober Saucen GmbH.

"There was nothing from Alexander Schober about it in the press. But then the news spread through the media world. Schober AG acquired the rights to your body-and-stomach fast food chain for the impressive sum of 5.8 million Swiss francs. Not bad for a startup."

Carmen, delicate, blonde-haired, almost a meter sixty tall, or short, depending on how you look at it, rolled her eyes in confirmation. It's hard to imagine that this ethereal creature ate meat at all, let alone heavily seasoned chicken wings from a cardboard box, with country fries and rich sauces on the side. But she sent evidence in the form of a selfie to Loretta via WhatsApp whenever she visited her boyfriend in London.

"I know, I've been collecting everything about Wings to Heaven since they planned to come to us. I basically have the whole history." Carmen smiled proudly, opened her laptop and added the information with the additional comment that the Schober company from Niederbuchsiten not only holds the rights for expansion in the DACH region, but is also intended to become a sauce supplier.

"Daniel Burmann, partner and CEO of the company, wants to shake up the fast food industry, which he sees as too dominated by the big players. He wants to break new ground with his Schober AG. Faster, more profitable and more standardized, that's his motto," summed up Carmen.

"He said that? So provocative? That doesn't sound very Swiss."

"Bingo, he also comes from Germany, as it says in an article in the Handelszeitung. I'll send you the links.

He also wants to expand as quickly as possible into Germany and Austria."

"That's strange," Loretta was skimming through an article on her laptop. "Here is an interview with Alexander Schober in the food magazine in which he expresses his enthusiasm for the new sauce concept, which is essentially a commitment to sustainability. It's also supposed to have health-promoting ingredients. If this is well received, then it should be adopted for the entire system. But here the tenor of the approach is more *step-by-step* and we are talking about slow food. However, the sauces also seem to attract new prospective franchisees abroad who are very enthusiastic about Swiss Quality, it says at the end of the article." Loretta looked at Carmen to double down.

"Then there are very different opinions at Schobers. A completely new wind is moving into the company. Schober AG, a traditional Swiss company with regional suppliers and quality products, avoided bankruptcy five years ago and was resurrected with new money. Now it becomes a partner in a fast food chain. Our client Burmann is thus securing a new line of business and a new source of sales for sauces and dips. Well, I would let Schober disappear if he is more of a fan of slow food. Especially when Schober has made an innovative breakthrough with the sauces. Hmm, health-promoting sauces. I can hardly imagine it, but I'll probably find out more about it from Daniel Burmann this afternoon. Let's see."

"Oh, Carmen. Tomorrow morning, I will meet Schober's wife. She comes to our office with her sister. I have to find out more about Alexander Schober, what kind of person he is - hopefully he really still is. There appears to be no sign of a kidnapping and no report of an accident. It's all very strange."

Loretta couldn't figure it out yet, but she felt pretty hungry after all the talk about food.

"I'll stop by the sushi shop at the train station. Should I bring you something?"

"Yuck. Raw, cold fish wrapped in this rice and seaweed banderole. No thanks. I brought something from home."

"Before I forget, be so kind as to find out exactly where in London the International Meeting for Detectives is taking place and book a hotel nearby for Lars and me."

Carmen put on her most innocent look. "Double or single room?" Loretta turned around again at the front door.

"Single room or, where the room is the size of a closet, a double room."

Carmen let out a meaningful "Aha."

"Do I hear a certain undertone there? My dear Carmen, you did that to me last time with that mini room. I'll leave any ambiguity at that. You know when I'm hungry, I'm not human - or what does that commercial say?"

"I think you are you, even when you're hungry," Carmen giggled. "That's the great thing about you!"

"Arrivederci!" With a laugh, Loretta went to the door. She liked it when the tone in the office was relaxed. And Carmen was an asset. She had been her assistant for a year and a half. Resilient, clever and tough, which helped her in her research and also in the team. Carmen Cadruvi, although only in her mid-twenties, could nonchalantly adapt to different characters and situations and, with her dry humor, even made Lars' assistant Morita laugh - well, subtly smile. Especially when she brought his Japanese R sound into the Graubünden roll. Humor was vital for Loretta. And that despite the fact that she worked in an industry that revealed the depths of humanity. It was probably some kind of compensation. But she didn't want to waste any deep thoughts on it now. Especially not when she could concentrate on the different sushi combinations on the display.

6

"Mr. Burmann will be with you immediately, Mrs. Lombardi." A busty blonde in a slightly trashy look accompanied Loretta to the seating area.

"Is there anything new from Mr. Schober? Oh God, it's all so terrible." That said, Jasmin Bolliger, as her sign at the reception said, answered her own question, because she didn't really seem to be waiting for a response.

"Can I offer you something? A coffee or water?"

"Thank you, both are welcome." Loretta took off the coat that she had put on for the short sprint from the car to the main entrance. She basically forgot about umbrellas. She ran a practiced grip through her long hair to collect the drops and twist a loose braid at the nape of her neck. The drive to Schober AG in Niederbuchsiten was rainy and tiring due to the hectic overtaking people on the motorway. Loretta enjoyed driving her blue car - or Mazi, as Fred called it - but in heavy rain or worse, snow, the car was a disaster. For the umpteenth time she thought about buying a more solid car. One that contained the three S's: slim, sporty and safe. With these thoughts and the assurance that she really had her notebook with her, Daniel Burmann approached her. A sporty figure in a shirt and cargo pants, medium height, bearded, around his late forties. His shoes squeaked unpleasantly, either due to poor workmanship or because they hadn't been paid for. Her grandmother would have said the latter. With such wisdom from her German maternal grandmother and the harsh prophecies from her paternal Nonna, Loretta had amassed a considerable repertoire of parables and sayings for every occasion.

Daniel Burmann greeted Loretta busily and led her to the elevator. His office was at the top of the third floor. Another version of Jasmin Bolliger, also blonde and curvy but less trashy, had just put down a tray of drinks.

"Sorry," came Jasmin Two, who, as it later turned out, was called Evelyne Kaltenbrunner. She laboriously dried the small lake of coffee from the saucer.

"It's okay," Loretta remarked, who was able to follow the clumsy movements thanks to the foamless coffee. It didn't seem like it was her day-to-day job.

"Thank you, Evelyne!" came back like an order from Burmann, who had moved from the desk towards Loretta. Loretta's hair literally stood on end, the situation was so tense. She poured all the ingredients into the black sadness called coffee and watched the scene as she stirred. Evelyne Kaltenbrunner had left with a withering look at Burmann. It was almost stage ready.

"It's good that you were able to come so quickly. I have little time, Mrs. Lombardi. Everyone here is a little nervous right now. There is a lack of staff. And Alexander, Mr. Schober, has been missing since Wednesday evening. That's inexplicable! We are in absolutely important negotiations with potential partners in Germany. It looks nothing like Alexander. "He's very old school, he's always reliable," Daniel Burmann said.

"May I ask you, if there was anything unusual or a disagreement with your business partner and colleague? Mr. Schober is your colleague, isn't he?"

"Yes, of course. We have a relationship of absolute trust. Maybe not quite in the Swiss colleagues sense, that we are friends. We don't go to the slopes together or have the same hobbies. There's quite a difference in age between us. But we get along and go out to eat every now and then. Whatever you do. And we have a clear division in business. I am responsible for strategy, cooperation and expansion and he is responsible for product development and certification."

After Daniel Burmann had stared primarily at his shoes while telling the story, which had probably already been paid for but actually looked unfashionable and cheap, he now turned directly to Loretta when briefly introducing his job, as if he wanted some form of confirmation.

"I already understand your division of responsibilities. Are there points on which you don't understand each other?"

Burmann seemed slightly irritated. "It's none of your business. But, yes, certainly, Alexander is a little, how should I put it, a little more cautious when it comes to expansion. He was initially against buying the license rights! A young company, and then from England, with crazy design, as he called it. He watched photos on Instagram and films on TikTok after I showed him how innovative the chain is on social media. To date, Alexander only knew about Instagram through hearsay. Oh well! And TikTok... He was already having a hard time with his laptop." Burmann took a short break, which Loretta took advantage of.

"He has pretty precise ideas about the time horizon for the launch of the new sauces. So everything step-by-step."

"Why do you think that? Alexander may sometimes express himself a bit cautiously, but in the end, he was very convinced of the licensing system and our approach. After all, it's about Schober AG."

"But he doesn't find everything convincing, does he?"

"Our figures show that we cannot continue like this. Two steps forward, one step back. We have to grow. Grow fast. The bank also wants to see results. And stop with the sauces. This tinkering with the sauces cost me nerves. But in the end, he somehow hit the mark! In any case, we have current inquiries, including from a large partner in Germany who is not only interested in Wings to Heaven but in exactly these new sauces."

"What's so new and health-promoting about it?" Loretta tried to neutralize Burmann's angry mood.

"First and foremost, the sauces are significantly lower in calories than those previously used at Wings to Heaven. The taste is even more intense. I have no idea whether it's because of the proteins or what, at least they're the door openers, to put it in modern German. Sauces that act like strength food, are good for building muscle and for the brain." Burmann illustrated the benefits by tensing one upper arm and tapping his biceps and then his forehead. Which gave the whole thing a slightly weird note.

"In terms of marketing, it will be amazing. I was told by our marketing agency that this goes in the direction of bio-hacking. You could also say body optimization, but that sounds very old school?" Burmann was now in motion.

"I invested five years and a lot of money to make something out of this company again. To bring them forward. With Wings to heaven we have a turbocharger! We have a scalable system and we can sell our top products through it. The English are thrilled. In addition to the rights for the DACH region, they guarantee us the supply of the entire system. The system is growing, I can tell you that! Now Alexander has disappeared. This means that the urgently needed innovation potential to continually develop new flavors is missing. That was Alexander's turn. These perspectives are of course interesting for our franchisor and our potential business partners! We're talking about completely different conditions." Daniel Burmann turned to Loretta with a bright red face. His tone oscillated between aggression and dismay.

"Things were just going perfectly. We were in the pilot phase with the products. Alexander made improvements and developed new variants almost every day. Some things he wrote down, others he had in mind. He wanted to sort everything out again. That's why he went to Ticino."

"And are there any notes from Mr. Schober about this? Or did they disappear with him?"

"I have found nothing. That's the problem. Nothing. I feel like an idiot."

"Who knew that Alexander Schober was traveling to Ticino? And perhaps also about what he was planning to do there?" Loretta studied Daniel Burmann as he sat slumped in his chair. There was nothing left of his slightly arrogant attitude.

"Just Mrs. Kaltenbrunner and Mrs. Bolliger – just in case, if one had to reach him. Otherwise, it was nothing special. Alexander often went to Ticino for the weekend. Nobody cared. But he was always available. When a telephone appointment came up, he was prepared as one can only be prepared. Do you understand?" Burmann looked at Loretta blankly.

"I would like to see the workplace of Mr. Schober, is that possible?" Loretta was already standing up to emphasize her request.

"You won't find anything there, but please, follow me." Burmann led Loretta into the laboratory on the first floor. It looked like a clinic. Everything was extremely bright, a white coat hung right next to the door and a neatly tidy desk was set up, also white like the walls, only the chair stood out with its blue padded surface. A glass front revealed a kitchenette and various shelves with identically shaped containers and handwritten labels.

"This is Alexander's empire. His job is here, but his real job is there."

Burmann tapped the glass and pointed to the kitchen and – it seemed – the experimental area.

"As always, he left everything neat and tidy. You are welcome to take a look around. I have to go to a meeting. If you have any further questions, please contact me - preferably by email or on my cell phone." Burmann handed Loretta his business card and disappeared with a short greeting. Loretta sat down on Alexander Schober's desk chair and tried to get a picture of him.

"So, Mr. Schober, you seem to be very disciplined. Even the chair is set perfectly straight," thought Loretta, opening the various drawers of the desk. They contained the typical office supplies, writing tools, a pad, a calendar, nothing flashy. A red hair tie and a tie were the only atypical items on the bottom shelf. Lost in thought, Loretta took the hair tie and stretched it between her thumb and forefinger. A faint scent emanated from the hair tie. Weak, yet intrusive and somehow familiar.

"Well, that's definitely a feminine touch that's lying dormant in the desk." Loretta put the hair tie in a small bag and inspected the kitchen or the laboratory, whichever was more appropriate. Everything indicated that it had been used a lot, burnt-in splashes on the hobs, discoloration on the work surfaces, but everything was cleaned and clearly arranged, even the small notes with the properties of ingredients were stuck in rows on the fronts of the shelves. There was also a white coat hanging on a clothes rack, although it showed signs of use. Interior and exterior pockets were empty except for one tablet in a cut-out piece of blister pack. It was not clear what medication it was. Loretta took this too, made notes and left Alexander Schober's empire.

"Mrs. Bolliger, I have another question."

"Of course, Mrs. Lombardo."

"di, Lombardi. When Mr. Schober left the office in the morning, did you notice anything else? Was he different than usual?" Jasmin Bolliger pondered.

"No, not exactly." Then she leaned forward a little towards Loretta, accompanied by a heavy, patchouli-like scent that had nothing in common with that of the hair tie, as Loretta stated.

"Well, I don't mean to have said anything, but he was kind of nervous. He asked whether Mrs. Kaltenbrunner was in the house." Jasmin Bolliger now placed her ample breasts on the reception counter and signaled to Loretta to come closer.

"Well, I'm pretty sure. There was something going on between them." She looked at Loretta with pleasure, sure of the curiosity she had now created. She played with the ribbon on her blouse, inevitably drawing attention to her cleavage.

"Incredible, between the two, Alexander Schober and Evelyne Kaltenbrunner?" Loretta acted conspiratorial.

"So you know, Evelyne is already taking everything she can get. I mean, it's none of my business, but... First she had an affair with Burman. And when she couldn't end up with him anymore, she turned to old Mr. Schober. At first, I almost felt sorry for him because he is always so decent and always thinks about the company. Then, Evelyne comes along," Jasmine Bolliger looked around briefly, scanning the surroundings for possible listeners, and then continued: "and wraps him around her finger. The old gentleman, Mr. Schober, really blossomed. They were in his lab together and ..."

"Mrs. Bolliger, if you would be kind enough, Mrs. Windscheid is waiting for Mr. Senn to call back. Can you follow up again! And is Mrs. Kaltenbrunner back? We want to start the meeting!" Daniel Burmann harshly appeared out of nowhere.

"Mrs. Lombardi, I hope you make quick progress. Please keep me informed." Visibly annoyed, Burmann dashed off again. Jasmin Bolliger dutifully apologized and picked up the phone. Loretta said goodbye and signaled that she would return again. The rain had subsided except for a few scattered drops. Loretta stepped outside the door as a black SUV drove past at a brisk pace and headed into a parking lot. Evelyne Kaltenbrunner came quickly towards Loretta.

"Mrs. Kaltenbrunner, nice to meet you again. I have a few questions. It's about Mr. Schober."

"I'm sorry, but I have to go to a meeting. I'm already late. Time has slipped away from me. Make an appointment through Mrs. Bolliger. Sorry, I have to."

During these staccato-like sentences her facial features changed, her entire demeanor even changed between innocence and concentrated control. With that she rushed past Loretta, trailing an intrusive scent of perfume behind her. Almost a little scary, thought Loretta as she sat back in her car and looked back on Evelyne Kaltenbrunner's performance. Loretta pulled the hair tie out of the bag and sniffed it. "Fits."

7

"Mrs. Lombardi is waiting for you, please follow me into the meeting room." Carmen led Elsie and her sister into an airy, bright room whose windows overlooked Lake Zug. Elsie didn't miss the opportunity to inspect everything carefully. As they passed an office, she caught a glimpse of well-ordered chaos. There was no other way to describe it, because there were piles of magazines, documents, bits and bobs piled up here and there, but somehow it looked like a system. She couldn't see anything else as her attention was captured by an illustration in a large glass frame. A female comic character who ripped open her uniform jacket, Superman-style, to display a 40 on her chest. Unfortunately, she couldn't read exactly what was written in a speech bubble. Something with Brenda or something like that. It's a shame, it was all so exciting. And if the reason for her being here weren't so sad, she would rather want to know about everything that she otherwise only knew from the countless crime novels that she devoured.

"Grüezi Mrs. Schober. Grüezi Elsie, sorry, Mrs. Caruso."

"It's okay, Mrs. Lombardi. Elsie is fine, after all that is our stage name *Luigi e Elsie – frutta e verdura*." Elsie grinned briefly before she again presented herself appropriately for the situation and made herself somewhat comfortable on the red upholstered designer chair with her 30 kilos of added value. The two sisters couldn't have been more different. Bernadette Schober, tall, slim, distant-looking, with admirable long white hair, looked like one of those senior models in her combination of blue dress and matching cardigan. Elsie, small, round and rosy, seemed down-to-earth and compassionate with her mottled gray-brown short hair.

"Mrs. Schober, thank you very much for coming here. I can imagine that you are very worried. But maybe I can help you find your husband." Loretta tried to catch Bernadette Schober's gaze, but she stared out the window, lost in thought. Elsie took advantage of the break and wanted to mediate.

"Bernadette hasn't heard anything yet. Alexander seems to have been swallowed up by the earth." She looked at her sister.

"Mrs. Lombardi, he doesn't have a girlfriend, if that's what you believe. I didn't give him the opportunity to do that either. We've been together for 40 years now. Everyone knows their responsibilities.

My husband is a good guy, an honest man. Sometimes perhaps too honest." The sentences came as calmly as if Mrs. Schober were explaining to a caretaker how to treat the plants in the front garden.

"Can one be too honest?" asked Loretta.

"Maybe too open. Too correct. That's more accurate. Alexander always wants to do everything right."

For a woman who hadn't heard from her husband in almost a week, it all sounded very formal. The fact that she herself brought up the topic of a possible girlfriend could mean that she knew something and went straight ahead with it. Or she effectively couldn't imagine it. "Because what shouldn't be, can't be" Loretta mentally quoted Christian Morgenstern, the German poet. Elsie shifted in her chair like a child who also wanted to say something.

"Will you be able to do something for us?" she asked. "Luigi and I are very grateful to my brother-in-law for many things. He once helped us a lot when business wasn't going well. A fine person. A little absent at times." She noticed the embarrassment of her statement and covered it up by taking one of the delicious amaretti that Carmen had brought in with the coffee.

"May I ask you, if there were any problems at your husband's company? Is that why he withdrew at least once?"

"My husband's company ... But that's history. When Alexander and I got married, I basically married the Schober Saucen GmbH company. Or how should I say. It was the evenings and weekends when the children asked when dad was coming home. Whether they have to try something from his kitchen again." Bernadette Schober spoke more to herself than to Loretta.

"Do we have to try those boring sauces again? Aren't we allowed to just eat burgers with real ketchup like other children? It was Melissa, our daughter, who didn't like my husband's healthy diet. Things are different today, when she has children of her own. Lukas is more like my husband, doesn't eat meat, eats little at all and when he does, he analyzes everything that's on the plate. Do you have children, Mrs. Lombardi?"

Loretta was caught off guard by the unexpected question and was taken aback. "No, I have no children. That wasn't my path."

"Alexander didn't really feel comfortable with his role as a father either. He treated the children more like colleagues. Partners who should try his latest inventions and taste what spices are in it, whether it is too creamy, how it behaves in the mouth." Bernadette Schober laughed briefly, then turned her gaze towards Loretta again. "But they both adored him."

"Mrs. Schober, I am investigating on behalf of Mr. Burmann. He wants to do everything he can to find your husband. How do you feel about Mr. Burmann?"

"How should I relate to him? I should be grateful that he saved the company. But sometimes I wonder if that was really the best solution. I certainly don't know much about business, but if Alexander was previously very attached to his work, now he was even more involved. He was obsessed with inventing something new. Something that would bring back the company's old glory. He wanted to be responsible for that himself."

At the last words, Bernadette Schober's mood changed instantly. The objectivity with which she had spoken about her husband so far gave way to a brief and barely perceptible surge of emotion. Loretta handed her a glass of water, which she acknowledged with the slightest nod of her head. Elsie Caruso stuck to the amaretti and held back.

"Alexander was heartbroken when the company was virtually on the brink of bankruptcy. He was the third generation to run the company. He saw Lukas and Melissa as successors. But unfortunately he didn't think enough about the economic side. Schober products were too expensive compared to the many convenience products. I still remember how he came home one evening and complained bitterly that an old friend no longer wanted to order from him. For that very reason."

"And how did your husband become aware of Daniel Burmann?"

"It was rather the other way around. Mr. Burmann had heard of Schober Saucen GmbH. He saw great opportunities for the company. He wanted to reorganize and expand. He already had precise plans on how he could transfer the former family business to Schober AG and make it successful again.

"And how did your husband react to that?"

"I told you he was broken. He was like behind a glass wall. He was there, but not right reachable. Then agreed to everything because he didn't want to look like a loser in front of the children. Things only seemed to go better when he realized he was needed. That his ingenuity was needed. From then on, he was back in his element." Bernadette Schober adjusted herself in the chair and looked at Loretta penetratingly for the first time.

"He spent many nights in the laboratory again. Like before." Bernadette Schober looked stone-faced.

"He also visited Ticino several times to think through his formulas or, as he said, to *recycle ideas*. I then stayed at home. He didn't have time for me after all. I could have gone alone."

"Mrs. Schober, forgive me for asking, but can you think of a reason for your husband's disappearance? Did something develop in connection with the new assignment that was difficult."

"Mrs. Lombardi, nothing is easy for my husband. He's a five!"

Elsie, who had been following the conversation with interest, intervened.

"My sister is intensively involved in numerology. You just take your date of birth and add it up. I was born on March 7, 1965.

That adds up to 31 and you add it up again – or what do you call it?"

"You're making the cross sum." came Bernadette Schober.

"Anyway, I'm a four. Always reliable." As if in confirmation, Elsie smiled at her sister. Warm-hearted and loving.

"You have to explain that to me, Mrs. Schober. How does a five make a difference?"

"Full of creativity, thirst for development, but also self-doubting, independent and freedom-loving. That's why it makes no sense to accompany him in such phases. When we were newly married, I thought we could share thoughts like that. But after 40 years of marriage, I understand that it doesn't work. He's just a five!" That seemed to be the end of the matter. But she added almost in a whisper: "But the fact that he just stays away without getting in touch is new. This is not our agreement."

8

Carmen dissected all the information they had obtained so far on the Schober case and entered all the data into the database's internal profile: Alexander Schober (AS), Swiss, 64 years old, married to Bernadette Schober, 2 adult children named Melissa and Lukas, living in Aarau and Basel.

On Wednesday, April 2nd, around 11 a.m., AS drove towards Ticino. At around 3:00 p.m., after spending time in the "Stella del Nord" espresso bar in Ascona, he called his wife on his cell phone and then wanted to drive to his house in the Maggia Valley. She hadn't heard from him since. According to an acquaintance named Beat Hagmann, AS arrived at the house in Ronchini around 4 p.m. Beat Hagmann, something of a factotum, manages the house when AS is not present.

The business partner Daniel Burmann tried to reach AS by phone on Thursday morning, April 3rd, at 9 a.m. But AS was not available then or on the following days. Beat Hagmann drove to the Schobers' house at lunchtime on Thursday, April 3rd.

There was no evidence of a burglary, accident, kidnapping or another crime. AS's car was in the garage at the house in Ronchini. AS's cell phone has been switched off since his last call. It is not possible to locate the cell phone. A missing person report has been filed with the police. A search has not yet been launched because there is no immediate threat.

Pling! Carmen looked at a WhatsApp message from Loretta. "I'm on the way to Ticino to stop by Stella del Nord. Please try to find out everything about Daniel Burmann and Alexander Schober. There are inconsistencies. I'll get back. Loretta."

9

Loretta rolled down the windows in the car and took a deep breath. How she loved moments like this. She had barely left the Gotthard Tunnel towards Ticino when it cleared up. In half an hour she would be at her favorite café in Ascona. She had to make up her own mind.

"Loretta, Bella, good to see you! Like always?" As if she were ordering a double espresso every day at this time, Herbert had already started the piston coffee machine. One of the few small bars that had a Bezzera machine.

"So, what mission are you on today?" Herbert briefly wiped the already sparkling counter before serving Loretta an espresso.

"Wonderful! This espresso really deserves its name. Herbie darling, you are not only the best barista, but also the oracle of Ascona! What's new? Do you know anything about the missing person? This Mr. Schober?" Loretta felt alive. Caffeine and even the hint of Italianità were her personal amphetamines.

"He came here every now and then and always sat over there and read the *Neue Zürcher Zeitung*," Herbert pointed to a table for two right by the window.

"Ordered a Café Crème and a still water. Always the same. He behaved like a civil servant."

Loretta looked at the ambience of this small bar with the eyes of a detective. Five small tables, either with two or three chairs, were lined up along the window front. The central area was the counter, where most of the guests usually hung out to have a chat or simply to fit in.

"And did he always come alone?" asked Loretta, who was surprised that Schober appreciated a good coffee when the brew in the company was hardly drinkable.

"No, sometimes he was here with his wife, such a cool, silent one. The room temperature then went down at least five degrees each time. Thank God she was only there rarely and that was a long time ago. Herbert knocked the coffee grounds out of the flask as if to confirm his statement.

"So, how were they together? Harmonious?"

"No, that would be too much of a feeling. Each individual was just for himself. She was reading a book and he was reading the newspaper. They weren't unfriendly towards each other, just incredibly wooden. She always ordered tea, peppermint tea. To be honest, I was surprised when this siren appeared here. I definitely wouldn't have believed him to do that. But he probably doesn't either!"

"What do you mean? What kind of siren?" Herbert's bar was an Italian gem, but even after all these years he was still North German, as the name of his bar, Stella del Nord, also expressed it. Strangely enough, he was still very well integrated. This could have been due to his reserved manner and the dignity that he radiated with his gray, well-groomed, longer hair and the trimmed full beard. The term siren also went with it!

"A blonde poison. Handsome, but very possessive."

"What makes you think possessive?"

To demonstrate, Herbert grabbed Loretta's forearm and looked at her sternly.

"How would you interpret that?"

"But hello!" Loretta instinctively tore herself away. "That's when things really got going! Did you hear what they were talking about?"

"I would say it was maybe something relationship-related."

"What, do you think he had an affair in addition to his cool wife?" Loretta took a sip of water and pressed for more information.

"Yeah, well, he didn't like her surprising him here though."

"They both didn't come here together?"

"No, he was alone and had ordered his place setting as usual. But this time without a newspaper. He had read some papers. There was another huge sleigh outside trying to get into a parking space. I thought I couldn't believe my eyes. This blonde maiden behind the wheel not only did it with flying colors, she also came in and headed straight for this Schober. For the first time I saw that the man could change color. He really had to pull himself together."

"Oh, Herbie darling, don't make it so exciting. What happened then?"

"She seemed a bit out of sorts to me. But I couldn't understand what they were talking about. You know it's not my style to indulge in such things. I just noticed that she was doing this strange act."

Herbert made signs of grabbing Loretta's arm again, but then stopped, smiled and continued:

"After a quick Prosecco she went off again. He leafed through his documents a bit, but only stayed for about a quarter of an hour. The poor guy seemed a bit off track to me. No wonder."

"Do you remember the approximate time when it happened?"

"That was last Wednesday, just after noon. I don't open until 2 p.m. on Wednesdays. And he came when the coffee machine was just warming up."

"Have you told anyone about this?"

"What? The thing with the girlfriend? No. Why should I add fuel to the fire? My goodness, maybe he had a little adventure. He shall. And why make his cool wife unhappy? If she doesn't know it yet, then she shouldn't find out from me. I'm not a fan of hers, but she's been through enough. Besides, no one asked me." With that, Herbert began wiping his glossy counter for the fifth time.

"The siren's giant sleigh, was it a black off-road vehicle with a Solothurn license plate?"

"Black SUV is correct. I don't know the license plate number exactly. I just watched her park in the narrow space."

"Thanks, Herbie darling. You helped me a lot." Loretta put a tenner next to the espresso cup.

"It's on the house, Loretta. And next time give yourself more time for private matters." Herbert winked at her.

"Grazie mille, my dear," Loretta smiled. She would have liked to spend more time here, but things had to be done. She checked her watch. Now it was time to step on the gas. In the literal sense, because she had made an appointment in front of the Schobers' house at 5 p.m. Mr. Hagmann would show her the house.

10

Beat Hagmann was already standing in front of the door fiddling with the lock when he turned around, slightly irritated.

"Mrs. Lombardi?"

"Yes, you are Mr. Hagmann, right?"

"Exactly, Beat Hagmann. Funny, I know that I locked it twice," he looked first at his bunch of keys and then, with a questioning face, at Loretta.

"When was the last time you were here?"

"Well, this morning, after Mrs. Schober told me that you would be coming this afternoon. I thought I'd check things out. I'll take care of everything a little bit when the Schobers aren't there," he looked at Loretta with his age-pale eyes. The slightly worn corduroy trousers and the oversized cardigan suggested that he would certainly welcome a little extra income.

"Then let's go in, maybe you'll notice something unusual, Mr. Hagmann."

They entered directly into the hallway, which wasn't actually a hallway because all the rooms led from the small one entrance square. Loretta thought it was very well thought out and practical. On the left was the guest toilet, on the right a staircase that led upstairs and at the front you immediately came into the living area, which was followed by an open kitchen. Beat Hagmann let his gaze wander. This gave Loretta the opportunity to immerse into the house with all her senses and imagine the Schobers in it. It was immaculately tidy. The furniture looked a bit thrown together, but there was a common denominator. And that was: We don't throw anything away. The old seating set, a television with a picture tube, which probably already broadcast in color, crocheted curtains, cut wine glasses on the glass shelf, photos of children, probably the Schober children Melissa and Lukas, and here and there traces of current life. Because there was ashes in the small fireplace, in the kitchen there was a stone-dried lemon in a ceramic bowl and there were open bottles of vinegar, oil and a good Barolo next to the bread bin, as Loretta stated.

"Mrs. Lombardi, something is wrong here. The photo is flipped. The photo of Mr. and Mrs. Schober. When I'm here in the living room, I have a ritual like that. I always greet them because from the photo they look directly in my direction when I come in. But now it's reversed."

"Perhaps you came across it this morning or a gust of wind knocked it over during ventilation?" Loretta looked at the framed photo. Bernadette Schober could be seen on it, her iridescent blonde-white hair had been loosely pinned up. She stood next to her husband, smiling, in a rather casual outfit. He joyfully held a large *papier-mâché key* in his hand.

"That was when they both moved in, in 1999. It took a while until the house became something livable. Mrs. Schober tackled things properly. I wouldn't have thought it possible, because she is so ..., so special." Beat Hagmann now stood next to Loretta and looked at the photo almost reverently.

"Special? What do you mean?"

"She is so fine. Comes from a family of pharmacists in Schaffhausen. She told me that once when I was helping her in the garden. She planted herb and flower beds there and told me a lot about the effects of natural remedies." He went to the window and pointed with his hand towards the garden, which still seemed a bit sleepy at this time of year.

"I can help myself there for my own use. Some things grow like weeds. I just have to be careful because there is also something poisonous in there. I have set up a small herbal pharmacy at home. That makes me independent of all these medications they want to prescribe me at my age."

"Then you have a good relationship with the Schobers." Loretta made it sound like a statement and not a question.

"Yes, of course. Very splendid people. It is completely inexplicable to me what happened to Mr. Schober. He's been here a lot lately, often alone, but he didn't seem depressed. On the contrary, he was sometimes even a bit exuberant, in a way I didn't even know him. Just thought his wife was so busy with their daughter, who's expecting another child soon."

"Mr. Hagmann, could we please take a look upstairs to see if you notice anything there too, now we still have good light."

"Sure, Mrs. Lombardi. Do you think something bad happened to him? Maybe he was even kidnapped?" Beat Hagmann climbed the unusually high steps somewhat unsteadily and turned to Loretta at the landing. His questions hung in the room.

"I'm collecting all possible clues at the moment. I have to get a picture."

The bedroom was dark and cool. Two large, triangular windows with perfectly fitted, almost closed blinds dominated the room. The little light that fought its way through the slits in the blinds revealed silhouettes of furniture and indefinable objects.

"One moment," said Beat Hagmann. He was definitely familiar with the house. Without turning on the light, he had already activated the switch for the automatic blinds.

"My goodness, what a view," Loretta looked at Beat Hagmann in amazement. He smiled gently and almost proudly, as if it were a castle that he was responsible for giving guided tours of every day. The bed was ideally placed, as you had the window front in front of you and could see the forested mountains to the left and the valley that seemed to dissolve into the hazy horizon. The Schobers may have had a marriage that was getting old, but anyone who treated themselves to this view from their bed definitely had a sense of romance.

"And, Mr. Hagmann, do you notice anything that's different?"

"No, I can't pinpoint anything specific. It's more of a feeling that someone was here. I always just take a quick look to see if everything is okay and I'm not up here every time because sometimes - especially when the weather changes - my bones hurt. And then the steps."

He shuffled into the adjoining bathroom as if to confirm. The neon lights flickered on. Loretta was now standing next to Beat Hagmann and was confronted with their two reflections. At this point at the latest, romantic feelings were over. The white-green light didn't just make Beat Hagmann look unhealthy and haggard. Loretta's eyes also seemed dull in the mirrored cabinet and her skin seemed strangely pale. The waxy, eggshell-colored shower curtain in the background probably contributed to this. The bathroom had the charm of a high school chemistry laboratory from the 1950s. Even the pale cosmetic bottles and jars seemed to be from that era. Loretta was happy when they were back in the bedroom. From there they went into the study, which had been converted into a multifunctional room.

"Did the Schobers have visitors often?" Loretta felt almost uncomfortable that she had asked the question in the past tense. This also made Alexander Schober's disappearance so absolute.

"Well, in the beginning their children accompanied them, of course, and later, when the two of them were studying, they helped here and there. Especially Melissa. She is more of a practical one. From all of them." Hagmann smiled and ran his hand over a solid wooden shelf that was slightly curved due to the numerous books.

"She can put up shelves, without instructions and a lot of talking. Now she is having her third child. She and her husband have their own construction business in Aarau, in the canton of Aargau."

"And then there is a son?"

"Yes, Lukas. He is a biologist. A quiet man, he does research, but I can't remember where or at which university. All I know is that he is very successful. Basel. Now it occurs to me, he's in Basel."

"Is that why Mr. Schober has been so exuberant lately? A third grandchild, successful children. A wonderful woman ..." Loretta left the sentence unfinished.

"I can't say for sure. Mr. Schober was always so friendly and would invite me for a glass of wine every now and then when he was alone here. Then we sat by the fireplace and he talked about the family and sometimes about his business. And I talked about Margot, my wife, who died three years ago, and about my daughter. She lives in Australia, you know. Those were lovely evenings." Beat Hagmann sat down on the office chair. Loretta placed herself on a chair opposite so that she was at eye level again.

"And when was the last time you had an evening like this?"

"It was still cold there, that was in February. Yes, exactly, it was the end of February. Mr. Schober said that his son might be staying in the house during the Basel carnival. He wanted to escape the hustle and bustle. He's more of a quiet person."

"And after that you saw less of Mr. Schober?"

"Yes, it was more between door and door, as they say. There were also quite a few visitors there. However, his son didn't come."

"Did you know about the visitors?"

"Yes, I had probably seen Mr. Burmann twice. He is Mr. Schober's business partner and he was there before. And then there was a young lady there. I hadn't seen her before, but she probably also works for Mr. Schober. However, I forgot the name. But she was reckless. As if she owned the house. I then quickly left again. I had only handed in the trade invoice from the roofer. The winter caused quite a bit of damage this time."

"So it was probably a business meeting. Was it a friendly agreement?"

"I wouldn't say friendly. Not unfriendly either. Busy, just like Mr. Burmann always is when I see him. I don't think he's ever looked at his surroundings. Even when I met him once on his walk with Mr. Schober.

Mr. Schober has a fixed route that he follows so that he can always reach his favorite viewpoints. But Mr. Burmann paid no attention to the Maggia or the panorama; he talked and talked to Mr. Schober. At least that was my impression when I saw them from afar. And Mr. Schober didn't like the fact that I met them and the mood was somehow upset.

Loretta's phone vibrated. A message from Carmen. "Mr. Hagmann, I don't want to keep you any longer, but can you tell me when Mr. Burmann and the blonde lady visited and whether you saw anyone else afterwards?"

"Yes, that was during carnival time. In the middle of February. On Monday, when Lukas actually wanted to be there because he didn't want to witness the morning prank at 4 a.m. I was quite surprised not to see him, but the three of them. After that I was only there once more because Mrs. Schober had informed me that her husband wanted to come on April 2nd. and that I should let the cleaning lady, Signora Agnelli, know. Yes, and then of course several times in the last few days since Mr. Schober disappeared. The police were here once and asked questions similar to those you asked, Mrs. Lombardi. Did I notice anything unusual?

Mr. Burmann was also here and was looking for something."

"Oh yes, did he say what he was looking for?"

"Yes, an express shipment, an A4 envelope. We then searched the house together. But there was nothing."

"I would like to take a look at Mr. Schober's car."

"Of course." Loretta followed Beat Hagmann down the stairs after he had put everything back in the usual order.

"Use this to open the garage door and here is the car key. I think you won't find anything because neither the police nor Mr. Burmann noticed anything. It's terrible. What could have happened?"

The garage made a clear impression. Everything was somehow in its place, few car accessories, but more garden utensils, buckets, gloves, empty flower pots, watering cans. From first impressions, everything seemed to have not been used for some time, even though it was long past time for gardening. There was definitely nothing unusual in the car. Loretta looked through the console mechanically: there was a gas voucher from a retail chain, then two business cards from restaurants in the area, a parking receipt, a card from a used goods dealer from Locarno and from an

Antonio Vivace, also from Locarno, another: sgomberiamo il tuo appartamento - We're clearing out your apartment.

"Those typical advertising cards that are stuck to your car window," thought Loretta. Recently there has been a card on her driver's door several times with the best price for her Mazi from a used dealer near Lucerne.

"What were they actually thinking? The car was pretty new." Loretta was happy to be back in her car. Alone with her thoughts. She waved to Beat Hagmann, who drove away in his rickety Golf. A really nice man, she thought, attentive, responsible and yet reserved when it came to anything too private. His observations were insightful. This express shipment must have definitely contained something important, but it seemed to have disappeared with Schober. But now she had to put the puzzle together.

A good meal and excellent wine were waiting for her at home. These were the best conditions. Loretta turned right off the road to get to the gas station. There were still around 150 kilometers to Lucerne, and there might be a shortage of gas. Unfortunately, many people seemed to have decided that. Loretta was just about to turn around again when she saw a black SUV with a Solothurn license plate in front of the gas station shop.

"Mrs. Kaltenbrunner, how nice to meet you here. My assistant, Mrs. Cadruvi, wanted to make an appointment with you today. Good thing it's working now. We're running out of time." Loretta was still a little out of breath. Finding a parking space, keeping an eye on Evelyne Kaltenbrunner and a quick trot to the shop.

"Who are you?" Evelyne Kaltenbrunner stared at Loretta, visibly irritated.

"Lombardi, Loretta Lombardi. I'm investigating the Alexander Schober case. We saw each other twice at work yesterday. Sorry, I thought you remembered me. But, of course it's all a bit much now. Can we sit there for a moment?" Loretta pointed to a combination of seats a little away from the hustle and bustle of shopping.

"Yes, if it doesn't take too long. I still have to go further."

"Mrs. Kaltenbrunner, I don't want to take up too much of your time, so I'll ask straight away. Are you having an affair with Alexander Schober?"

"What's that supposed to mean? How dare you?" Evelyne Kaltenbrunner rummaged in her handbag and snapped a tablet out of a blister pack.

"Sorry, but I have a headache." She quickly swallowed it down with a long gulp from a bottle of mineral water.

"I can imagine that. The uncertainty over such a long time. Almost a week without a sign from Alexander Schober. When was the last time you had contact with him?"

"I tried to reach him. I called him again and again, but the cell phone is switched off." Evelyne Kaltenbrunner stared at the table top.

"When was the last time you saw him?"

"Saw him? That was last Wednesday. When he drove to Ticino. We met briefly in an espresso bar."

"Oh, you didn't drive together? You are a couple, aren't you?" Loretta made another attempt.

"Alexander is still cautious." As she said the last word, she looked at Loretta with a dreamy look. Almost childlike.

"Cautious? Is he planning a future together for both of you? Did you talk about this in the bar?"

"Yes, Alexander would like to start again. With me. He will leave everything behind."

"But Mrs. Kaltenbrunner, you know where he is. Please tell me where he is, then this spook will end and everything will be sorted out."

Tears ran down Evelyne Kaltenbrunner's face. Out of desperation, fear or anger? It was definitely not possible to clearly analyze her condition at that moment.

"I do not know where he is. He can't let me down!" People turned around in shock. Evelyne Kaltenbrunner had drowned out the enormous noise in the shop.

"Mrs. Kaltenbrunner, I'm sorry. Calm down. We will find him. Everything will clear up." Loretta handed her a handkerchief and looked around soothingly. However, their eyes had already turned away again. Such outbursts were apparently nothing special.

"Is that why you went to Ticino? Did you want to be close to him?" Loretta tried to get Evelyne Kaltenbrunner's attention in a whisper.

"I walked our hiking trails. We went for a lot of walks. Alex and me. That was nice."

"Can I ask you something else, Mrs. Kaltenbrunner? Mr. Schober had documents with him when you met in the Espresso Bar. Do you know anything about the contents of the papers?"

Evelyne Kaltenbrunner had regained her composure to some extent. She wiped her eyelids with the tissue, smearing her eyeliner. "No, I don't know anything about that. Alexander always has documents with him. If something comes to mind, he has to write it down. Mrs. Lombardi, I'm dead tired. It must be because of the tablet. I won't be going back today, but will be spending the night in the area. I can't do two and a half hours now."

"May I help you? I can drive you to a hotel."

"Thank you, no need, I can handle it."

"If you hear anything from Alexander Schober, please let me know immediately. No matter when." As with the first encounter with Evelyne Kaltenbrunner, Loretta noticed her confused personality.

11

Loretta swirled the red wine in the glass, inhaled the aroma with her nose and then took a small sip. Wonderfully spicy, this Tuscan Chianti. Matches the osso buco with risotto. Signora Agnelli had given her a little tip for the gremolata, which Loretta sprinkled over the meat. Add a touch of grated orange peel and the taste becomes even more perfect. Loretta chewed with pleasure. Pleasantly soft jazz music could be heard in the background. She put off the thought process until the espresso. A ritual that had proved its worth.

"So, what do we have here?" Loretta said to herself, placing the espresso cup on the rustic long wooden table that led from the kitchen directly into the living room. There was already a large A3 paper on it with the names of everyone involved in the Schober case as well as their brief descriptions and connections to each other. Signora Agnelli, who in addition to cleaning and occasionally providing culinary delights in the Schobers' house for seven years, was happy to talk to Loretta about both. The phone call was conducted in spirited Italian and therefore a little louder, which had a very invigorating effect on the way back in the car.

Ultimately it turned out that there had been indications since the beginning of the year that a woman must have stayed there overnight who was not Mrs. Schober, nor her daughter Melissa. But Signora Agnelli wasn't entirely sure. Because she wasn't responsible for the laundry, except for the ironing. But she had a keen nose and it told her that there was a new scent in the house. A heavy perfume that wouldn't suit Mrs. Schober, let alone her daughter. If the latter is also heavily pregnant, you react very sensitively to scents. In doing so, Signora Agnelli verbosely circled back to her own three pregnancies, which had given her a wide variety of food cravings, but also an aversion to smells and even perfumes that she had previously loved. Then she thought about it again and said rather meaningfully that there was another Vitalità in the house. A sudden liveliness that she couldn't explain other than through another woman.

Loretta tried to imagine Evelyne Kaltenbrunner and Alexander Schober as lovers. Not only the massive age difference, definitely 30 years, but also the other constellation in the company and in general seemed to be a difficult prerequisite.

What could Evelyne Kaltenbrunner have to do with the disappearance? And what was wrong when she met him in the café in Ascona? Did he want to end the whole thing? Is that why she was so hysterical earlier? The fact that Bernadette Schober knew about this or at least suspected something was revealed by her vehement manner in the initial interview. Her husband didn't have a girlfriend, although that wasn't even up for discussion at the time. Was she putting, as the saying goes, her finger in the wound? In addition, she had not been to Ticino in the last four months. Because of the pregnant daughter, as she emphasized.

Then there was Daniel Burmann, who must have given Schober a lot of trouble when he announced the purchase of the franchise chain. A conceited fool, Loretta's grandmother would have said. But why should he let Schober disappear? He had what he wanted and more, because apparently Schober had promoted the sale of the licenses with the new sauces. However, not having the recipes for other variants in-house was negligent. What kind of urgent shipment was Burmann busy with? Schober had been missing for almost a week now. What did he have to do with this urgent shipment?

Loretta yawned loudly. She had to go back to Schober AG as quickly as possible. She had told Carmen that after reading her email about a fire that was said to have occurred near the Schober House in Ronchini. Two people were killed. A case of arson, but no indication that one of the dead was Alexander Schober.

"There's a lot going on in Ticino," Loretta thought, stretching and heading towards the bathroom. Not without first taking a close look in the hallway mirror.

"Well, Signora Lombardi, the osso buco suits you well! You can see it straight away! A jog tomorrow morning wouldn't do any harm." With these quietly spoken thoughts, she sucked in her stomach and looked at herself from the side.

"It's okay." And with that, the hint of sportiness was gone again. The pedometer from the fitness tracker had to suffice. She had a sporty disposition, but sport had to be subordinate to the pleasure principle. For her it was incomprehensible that one would be totally committed to a sport and would also build up pressure in one's free time. Her sporting preferences changed with the seasons, the occasions, the moods and the eating habits. Until recently, her relationships had been similarly varied. But that was now becoming too strenuous and was no longer compatible with her job. A certain amount of reassurance was good for her in this regard.

"Well, let's see what these numbers are all about ..." Loretta picked up the book that Nicole had recommended to her. If anyone knew anything spiritual, it was Nicole.

Nicole Wenger, who was actually a product manager in a food company, developed this second personality around 10 years ago and was working on building her own business with astrological evaluations and much more. Loretta had met her through a case related to her employer. Although it turned out that the accusation against the company was unfounded, for Nicole it was the initial spark to deal with influences whose explanations lay in the spiritual and symbolic. Since then, Loretta and Nicole have had a friendship that was full of tension due to the different characters and opinions, but also very meaningful. Loretta had a strong intuition that had served her well in many cases, but she was reluctant to admit it to the outside world. And so there were many discussions with Nicole, who knew Loretta's potential in this regard and recommended that she cultivate the spiritual side. She was even more enthusiastic when Loretta asked for a book recommendation on numerology.

"Loretta, my dear, you are a seven: full of optimism, joy of life and thirst for freedom! But you know that. I'll send you a link to my absolute favorite book," Nicole had told her energetically on the phone. Loretta leafed forward in the e-book and came across the five as if by chance. Fives, sixes and sevens are head people. Fives try not to get drawn into the whirlpool of feelings and events.

12

Blood ran down over the right hand, which was clutching at something rocky. It all seemed strangely detached and then clear again, followed by incredible pain as one tried to take a breath. In general, the chest seemed to be crushed in the middle, pressed against a rocky outcrop with bushes that had apparently ripped open the entire face. A streaky film in the eyes clouded the vision. Was it blood ? Thinking and acting was so incredibly difficult because everything kept blurring, not just the view, but also the conscious and unconscious, this world and the hereafter. Then some of the branches of the overhanging bush on which the first fall came to rest broke off. The second fall ended a good 600 meters lower. What was left lying there was a bloodied, lifeless bundle that only faintly resembled the person who had felt confident of victory an hour before.

13

"Mrs. Lombardi, you know I don't have much time. Production for our franchise chain is starting. New machines, even more powerful, fantastic to see. Now we just have to ensure meat production with the suppliers. But that's just a formality. We even do something for animal rights activists! We use the brother rooster chicks. Not long ago, the boys were shredded. But now they'll be pampered up a bit, then they'll have real meat on their bones."

Burmann rubbed his hands and laughed at his own humor. Loretta shuddered slightly. She did eat meat, but rarely and when she did, it was selected organic meat.

"What are the chicks fed with?" asked Loretta.

"With vitamins and, oh I don't know. Everything permitted. Not my area. I just ensure the supply chain and produce the corresponding sauces and dips. We're currently in the process of downgrading everything a bit. If Alexander leaves us in the dark, we'll have to improvise. A laboratory has analyzed the last sauces and now we're getting to the bottom of it. It may taste a little different, but it will be cheaper and we can still score points with our bio-hacking. "Let's go down here to the meeting room." Burmann made an inviting gesture to accompany him. His elation was almost palpable and in complete contrast to the last visit.

"Is there anything new from Alex?"

"Not specifically, but we have various clues." Loretta answered, looking around the puristically furnished meeting room.

"You know that Mr. Schober had an affair with Evelyne Kaltenbrunner?"

Burmann cleared his throat. "Yes."

"Why didn't you tell me that last time? At least that sheds a completely new light on the situation. Loretta tried to catch Burmann's gaze. But he spoke directly past Loretta, basically to the wall behind her. Loretta provoked by turning around briefly to press for an answer even more demandingly.

"I didn't want to make a big deal about it. But Evelyne and him. Well, you know, he threw his traditional man of honor attitude overboard and messed around a bit ..."

"How long had the relationship been going on? Weren't there problems, here at work and privately?"

"I think Alex got cold feet. In any case, it was all a bit too, how should I say, too close for him. Bernadette, Mrs. Schober, certainly noticed something too. After all, the two have been married for 40 years. At least Alex mentioned that he was planning a big trip with Bernadette. As a wedding anniversary surprise. Probably more of a *sponge-don't-know-it* kind of thing. Burmann suddenly became strangely talkative.

"Well, I don't care what people say here in the company. What counts for me is performance, not gossip. Everyone has a skeleton in the closet."

"Well, let's hope not, Mr. Burmann. There is also a story going around that you had an affair with Mrs. Kaltenbrunner."

"Did Mrs. Bolliger tell you that? I wouldn't be surprised. The scandal press made flesh. Evelyne Kaltenbrunner is not one of her friends. She embodies what Mrs. Bolliger would like. Sovereignty," Burmann literally spat out the word.

"Mrs. Kaltenbrunner has developed well over the last five years. She's not just my assistant, she takes care of the shopping and keeps an eye on everything. Disciplined this lax bunch and opened up new purchasing channels. Sometimes she might be too tough and employees like Mrs. Bolliger can't stand that."

"An exciting profile description. Have you been in a relationship with Mrs. Kaltenbrunner?"

"Have you been in a relationship with Mrs. Kaltenbrunner?" Burmann repeated the question irritably.

"There was something. Short. That's how it is. We had a great business meeting. It just went a bit beyond the sales figures. It didn't even last three weeks. It was nice, but I didn't want to jeopardize the employee relationship. She is more important to me as my right hand. Besides, it was a while ago now. I can barely remember."

"Did she see it that way too?"

"Evelyne? I think yes, she's tough. The fact that she went to bed with Alex was perhaps a little embarrassing, but if it was good for her." Burmann leaned back in his chair and looked Loretta directly in the eyes for the first time.

"Well, the relationship doesn't seem to be over. Mrs. Kaltenbrunner went to Ticino yesterday."

Burmann seemed taken aback. "What, have you seen both of them?"

"I met Mrs. Kaltenbrunner by chance last evening, at a gas station outside Ascona. She wasn't in good shape. Does Mrs. Kaltenbrunner sometimes have problems?"

"Evelyne is, how shall I put it? Evelyne is sometimes a bit unbalanced. She has had therapy. Something about trauma and depression. But she's well adjusted, as they say. She takes her pills regularly and this is how it works. Did she say anything to Alexander about where he might be?"

"No, she seemed more desperate that he wouldn't get in touch."

"Yes, that's typical Evelyne. She has to recognize when something is hopeless. It will be allright. First, she clings and then she lets go. In any case, it certainly gives her work the right drive." Burmann looked at the clock.

"Mrs. Lombardi, I have to go. Duty calls."

"I would like to speak to Mrs. Kaltenbrunner again. Is she back from Ticino yet?"

"You'll have to be patient. She took the day off."

"Can you please give me her cell phone number."

"Mrs. Bolliger will give it to you. Goodbye, Mrs. Lombardi. Let me know as soon as you hear from Alex." By his last words Burmann was already at the door and out.

"Unpleasant, simply unpleasant, this guy," thought Loretta, "but duty is duty and schnapps is schnapps" as her German grandmother would have said with a stoic expression.

14

"Buon Giorno, my dear." Lars smiled at Loretta over the rim of his teacup and pressed the start button on the coffee machine.

"You're fantastic, Lars. I urgently need a coffee." Loretta slipped past Lars into the small office kitchen and took a close look at Lars' teacup. "Green tea?"

"Would you like a little sample? This is a very rare Japanese green tea Sencha from the Chiran region of Kagoshima Prefecture. It is full-bodied and strong, slightly bitter, with a sweet note."

"I'll stick to the coffee for now." Loretta enjoyed grinding the coffee in the machine. Lars leaned casually in the doorframe. For her he seemed like a reincarnation of aliveness.

"My goodness, you look amazing, Lars."

"Thank you likewise. But something seems to be bothering you deeply."

"Unfortunately that's true, I have this Schober case, which wasn't actually a real case until now, but is now developing more and more into one."

"That sounds exciting and really like an Loretta case! Then let's hear it."

"Imagine that Alexander Schober, the former company owner, now only a minority shareholder, disappears without a trace in Ticino and all company business continues as usual. His motive is still completely unclear. Also, whether there is anything criminally relevant at all. He has been married for 40 years but was now involved with an employee. A relationship act is possible. However, there are no signs of any violent crime or anything like that. He simply disappeared. His ex-lover, who I met by chance in a parking lot in Ticino, was totally confused. Now both of them are no longer available."

"Well, maybe he's already left and she's following him. Or, she's giving him hell and he's withdrawn for a short while." Lars poured himself another green tea from his elegant Japanese teapot.

"Freddy Mouse would say that too. But that's somehow too simple. I have a strange feeling about this Burman. He is the managing director of the new AG that took over the bankrupt GmbH. He is our client, but somehow the whole situation works quite well for him now. He can pursue his goals without anyone constantly trying to come up with new ideas that cause additional costs." Loretta had a second coffee from the machine.

"You mean that Mr. Burmann gave us the search task as a pretense in order to distract from his true motives? That would indeed be unique. But in the franchise economy there is nothing that doesn't exist!"

"That could certainly be the case, although it would be very conspicuous to get someone out of the way because of it. Burmann is a complacent guy, but would he be capable of it? I don't know. If so, there must be more to it. And the relationship with Evelyne Kaltenbrunner seems to have had no deeper meaning for him.

"I think the other guy had a relationship with that woman."

"Lars, my dear, you are absolutely right. They both had something with her. That's the drama. Because, I think, that bothered Evelyne Kaltenbrunner. I can't really assess her yet, but she almost seems like she has borderline syndrome."

"Well, that's pretty tricky. That gives you another candidate who might have a motive."

"Well, yes ..., but there are still a few black holes in the whole thing. I have to think. Thank you very much, Lars, for listening. See you." And with that Loretta disappeared into her office.

15

Loretta tapped her fitness tracker on her wrist. 12:09 p.m., 5,234 steps. The number of steps could definitely be increased, she thought, and briefly assessed where she could still add more distance today. In just under two hours the appointment with the notary Pius Balmer in Lenzburg, from whom Schober had received the express shipment, was due. Jasmin Bolliger may have been a gossip, but her information was also valuable. Loretta thought about the previous morning meeting again. Evelyne Kaltenbrunner still couldn't be reached on her cell phone. After last night, that wasn't very reassuring. So now there were already two disappearances who seemed to have been swallowed up by the earth. Regula had asked the Ticino police department, but there were no clues from there either. Neither a crime nor an accident.

"Hello Hello". Carmen opened the ajar door to Loretta's office with a flourish. "I have to show you something!" She opened her laptop and pointed to the article from a local newspaper in Ticino. The headline read: *The real estate agency Gmeiner & Partner in Ascona is celebrating its birthday.*

"Take a look at the picture on the right. Couldn't that be Alexander Schober?" Carmen enlarged the photo, which became increasingly blurry, but still most likely showed the figure of Schober talking to another man. However, the latter could not be recognized as he could only be seen in part.

"Do we have a time frame?" Loretta wanted to know.

"The opening took place on Wednesday, April 3rd, in the afternoon. On the same day Alexander Schober disappeared."

"Great research, Carmen! Please find out if he was invited there and also the name of the other man. In fact, whether anyone knows anything about Schober's whereabouts."

"I'll do my best. However, I have to leave at 3 p.m. today."

Loretta looked a little puzzled, but then remembered that she gave Carmen early on Wednesdays. She had to get into the habit of giving Carmen a little more compensation time for the additional hours she was happy to invest in intensive cases.

16

"Grüezi, Mrs. Lombardi. What can I offer you? Coffee, tea, a water?" Pius Balmer, around 70 years old, a total charmer and of exquisite elegance, accompanied Loretta to a baroque-looking seating area.

"I'd be happy to have an espresso and mineral water". In this environment, Loretta thought, the coffee should be right too.

"Mrs. Waser, please be so kind as to bring us two espressos and some mineral water."

Mrs. Waser closed the door of the office, which had the dimensions of a dignified reception hall. And yet the cleverly arranged areas made it seem cozy. The massive desk, with artfully turned legs, stood right next to the window front, to the right of which there was a library, matching the desk, which went over the corner and took up the entire long side of the wall. From the seating area there was a view of an impressive number of specialist books and world literature. Balmer followed Loretta's gaze.

"My compensation. Literature keeps my soul in balance."

"I can understand that." Loretta was glad that she had chosen the light gray designer pants suit today.

Stylish and puristic, with a black blouse, she formed an exciting contrast to the ambience and to the conversation partner, who was wearing a suit with a matching, elaborately crafted vest from which a pair of delicate reading glasses peeked out. The seating arrangement was predetermined in that a leather folder was already lying on one of the two curved sofas, which clearly indicated Balmer's place. With a friendly gesture he invited Loretta to sit on the sofa diagonally opposite. Loretta ran her fingers over the solid burgundy brocade fabric of the sofa. It wasn't her taste, but it all fit together. Apparently, Pius Balmer was good in business.

"Dr. Balmer, thank you for arranging the appointment so quickly."

"Of course, Mrs. Lombardi. Alexander is not just a client. I can say that over the many years that I have supported the company in legal matters, we have maintained something of a collegial friendship."

Mrs. Waser, a delicate woman in her mid-fifties wearing a burgundy-colored shirt dress, had entered the room almost silently, placed the espressos and the mineral water on the table and left with a friendly smile. A perfect mimicry, not only in her behavior but also in her appearance, she was flawlessly adapted to her surroundings. Loretta felt like she had landed in a hand-colored black and white English film classic. Everything was a little out of time, calm and deliberate. Balmer seemed to read Loretta's mind.

"We are in a place steeped in history, Mrs. Lombardi. Over there, you can see the *Miller's house*, built in 1785, in the age of the cotton boom." Balmer pointed to the window front, with the impressive, almost floor-to-ceiling windows that provided a view of the historic building.

"Do you know that Switzerland was once an important cotton country and Lenzburg was characterized by wealth and prosperity? Other magnificent buildings also bear witness to this." Pius Balmer had leaned back a little, but then thought about the actual reason for Loretta's visit.

"Excuse me, Mrs. Lombardi, I am always enthusiastic about the city's history. This makes me a bit self-indulgent at times. But that's not why you came here. How can I help you?"

"Well, the history is quite interesting and I regret not having more time for it. But the time factor is precisely what is precarious in the current situation. I am investigating the disappearance of Alexander Schober. Various suspicions are growing. One of them relates to the recipes that Mr. Schober created and whose records disappeared with him. These seem to be very valuable for the company - at least they have resulted in very interested business contacts. Maybe there is a connection there. And then there was an express shipment from you on April 3rd, which Mr. Schober took with him to Ticino. It seemed to be of great interest to him."

Pius Balmer leaned forward and looked at Loretta intently. "And now you would like me to tell you what the papers were about? Well, you have to understand that I'm not allowed to reveal business internals without Alexander Schober's consent." He cleared his throat.

"But of course there are special circumstances that require a certain amount of information to be disclosed."

"Dr. Balmer, I would like to understand what happened to Mr. Schober and what the disappearance is all about. I perceive him as a conscientious and straightforward person."

Pius Balmer put on his reading glasses and picked up the leather folder that was lying next to him on the sofa, but left it closed. No doubt he was prepared.

"That's very nice, Mrs. Lombardi, and gets to the heart of Alexander's outstanding character traits. A month ago, he noticed that there were irregularities in the numbers at the company. More by chance, because he has nothing to do with the business management. He is active in development and only has to ensure that the planned figures in his budget are adhered to. And that too only peripherally. Mrs. Kaltenbrunner is now primarily responsible for purchasing within the framework of the franchise system, and Daniel Burmann is responsible for controlling development costs. You seem to know that Alexander Schober has created new sauces for the Wings to Heaven franchise system."

Loretta nodded, but refrained from commenting so as not to slow down Balmer's flow.

"He had seen what appeared to be an internal calculation of the costs of purchasing goods for the new location in Basel, which differed significantly from the calculations that formed the basis of the agreement with the Wings to Heaven franchisor. However, the sales, and thus the fees paid to the franchisor, did not show any noticeable irregularities, only the margin for Schober AG seemed to have improved significantly. Given the still low purchasing volume, for just two locations, this didn't seem logical. It was hardly to be expected that group advantages for the entire expansion could be perceived so early in this initial phase of Wings to heaven in Switzerland. Pius Balmer looked at Loretta over the rims of his glasses and paused to wait for her reaction.

"The sources of purchase could have changed and may no longer correspond to the quality?" Loretta wanted to know, took a sip of mineral water and tried to slow herself down. Because she actually wanted to get to the core faster.

"At least that's what it looked like. Alexander wanted to investigate. He felt obliged, as he was the one who not only rebuilt himself with the new recipes, but also significantly helped the company gain new momentum. Alexander told me that there were probably completely new sales channels and sales opportunities for nutritional supplements. He came across something new when developing the sauces. This could have a positive influence on the ability to concentrate and brain activity in general. Well, of course I found that very exciting too. At my age you're very perceptive." Balmer looked at Loretta with a hint of a smile, but then thought back to the situation.

"That must have made Mr. Burmann very happy. He's more driven by numbers."

"Ah, Mrs. Lombardi, you are well informed. Yes, but let's get back to the anomalies." Balmer opened the folder and leafed through a dossier.

"Alexander thought this animal rescuer idea with the brother rooster chicks was wonderful. That was another reason for him to really immerse himself in this new sauce concept. But then there were these number irregularities. Alexander had commissioned an expert report from me to have the sales products examined. He wanted to study the report in Ticino. Yes, that was on April 3rd."

"Did you speak to him afterwards?"

"No, he wanted to concentrate on this in peace and contact me when he returned."

"Can you please tell me more about Daniel Burmann. What kind of person is he?" Loretta nodded friendly to Balmer, who was pouring more mineral water.

"It's certainly not my place to judge that adequately. I got to know him better during the negotiations at the time, when he joined the company and subsequently in connection with patent matters. Without Mr. Burmann, Schober Saucen GmbH would probably have gone bankrupt. I cannot and do not want to decide whether it was the best decision. But the culture has of course changed significantly. While Schober Saucen GmbH used to be a guarantee of good quality and solidity, today it has ..., how should I put it, very modernized."

"Could you please explain this in more detail, Dr. Balmer"

"Well, Mr. Burmann is not very reserved in his statements. In general, his tone is, let's say, different. In doing so, he offends some people, whether in the company or with business partners. His promises are big, keeping them can then depend on many variables."

Balmer visibly tried to describe Burmann's character objectively and, as if to make up for what had just been said, it was reassuring.

"But you have to give him credit for that, he has brought the company forward again with the reorganization of Schober AG. It's not the first time he's done this either. In Düsseldorf, where he originally comes from, he rehabilitated a chemical company. He has a good hand when it comes to new orders and new connections. I can't say how ethical it is. I'm just surprised that he shows so much ethical awareness in Wings to Heaven."

"Well, the *Bother cock initiative* can of course be sold well in terms of marketing, together with the optimized sauces."

"You're certainly right, Mrs. Lombardi."

"If you say that the tone in the company has changed. How did Mr. Schober take that?"

"Oh, you know, Mrs. Lombardi, Alexander Schober is what you call a loner. He is happy when he can devote himself to his developments. I think he also wants to prove to his family that he can be successful and make money. He had spoken to Mr. Burmann about new ownership arrangements for the sale of these nutritional supplements. Maybe about a second company or a spin-off, but that wasn't ready yet."

"And Mr. Burmann? How did he see it?"

"As you say. He wants to earn money. My impression is that he is building up Schober AG so that he can sell it at a high price. Back then in Germany, he was denied the big money when reorganizing the chemical company. He worked in an advisory capacity and received only a commission, a very good commission, which also enabled him to join Schober."

"Is it conceivable that Alexander Schober would agree to a sale?"

"Alexander is emotionally one with the company. At least that was always the case. Legally he only has a minority stake, but he has granted himself the right to veto any possible sale. However, and this was discussed in our last conversation, the right of veto would be called into question. Burmann is a master. He would be able to legally turn it around so that a sale to financially strong buyers could increase the impact that the franchise system has with its special features and also make it possible to startup businesses to a greater extent."

Loretta emerged from the villa, Balmer's private residence with the office upstairs. She felt like a bit of a nest stain, after all she had asked Pius Balmer about Evelyne Kaltenbrunner at the end. What impression she had made on him. He thought she was bold, ambitious, but also a bit strenuous. Alexander raved about her, but had been avoiding turning the conversation to her lately. Loretta had hinted at rumors of a liaison between her and Alexander, which Pius Balmer vehemently denied. With this bad aftertaste in the otherwise insightful conversation, she entered the address of the laboratory on her cell phone that had prepared the report for Alexander Schober. Regula, with her charmingly determined manner, should take care of getting the results and, above all, their interpretations. Regula, it would be unimaginable if she actually quit next year. Loretta wished her well, but hoped that the tide would turn and she would stay. Because somehow she couldn't imagine Regula in this strange constellation of leadership position and relationship with the CEO. Time comes, advice comes, she thought, Il tempo lo dirà. At that moment, Loretta's cell phone vibrated. "Hello Loretta, are you sitting and can you stand an unpleasant message? I've just received the news that Evelyne Kaltenbrunner has been found dead. In the Maggia Valley."

17

"Loretta, amore mio!" Renzo Capuzzi, inspector of the Ticino police, sat down next to Loretta at the small bistro table and looked deep into her eyes.

"Good to see you, you look fabulous."

"Grazie, Renzo. Charming as always! Thank you for finding time so quickly." Renzo smiled and signaled to the bar, whereupon two double espressos were brought shortly afterwards. Renzo Capuzzi poured the contents of the sugar packet into the cup and stirred carefully. Loretta enjoyed the espresso with a touch of sugar.

"Loretta, how long has it been since we saw each other? Three years? Five years?"

"It's been a year and a half. It was about this kidnapping of the franchisor Maurizio Vitale. Luckily it turned out well."

"Loretta, my heart. I don't mean the Vitale case. I mean our ..." Renzo Capuzzi looked at her intently.

"Renzo, that was probably a good year ago now. And let me remind you, it was nothing! So nothing concrete. A wonderful evening. Luckily, I left before we got involved in something we might now regret." Loretta grinned. It really had been a wonderful evening.

They both met by chance. Loretta had gone to Ticino for a weekend and was strolling through Locarno when she met Renzo Capuzzi. He invited her to dinner because it turned out that he also liked cooking. They flirted heavily. And if Loretta hadn't noticed the photo of a little boy in the apartment, the evening would have been different. Renzo lived separately from his wife and son. And he suffered above all from the separation from his son, as he told her. Loretta's passion then fizzled out. She wasn't unhappy about it, because she was familiar with a relationship in this situation. It lasted three years, with endless ups and downs. Loretta was correspondingly relieved when she returned to her apartment and sat on the balcony with a view of Lake Maggiore. She really liked Renzo, his charm, his skill and his professionalism at work, but from a distance, her decision had been a good one.

"Perhaps our time will come again, Loretta." Renzo smiled, took the last sip of his espresso and, like Loretta, switched to professional mode.

"So you are investigating the case of the Schober company. So far, we have only recorded one missing person's report. There are no signs of Alexander Schober being kidnapped, nor any other crime. Only now this woman. Terrible. She fell from a ledge and was literally shattered. We don't know how it happened, yet.

"Wait, you're saying she fell down a rock face?"

"Yes why?"

"Oh, I had a dream a few days ago that really upset me. I haven't been able to place it yet. Am I falling down a rock or another person? Is it a metaphor for anything? But now something like this really happened. Terrible."

"Mia cara, you are very pale. Would you like a grappa?"

"No thanks. It's okay. But maybe I should cultivate my intuition more." Loretta opened her notebook. "Are there any clues as to what happened?"

"It could have been an accident. What's unusual is that she wasn't necessarily dressed for a hiking tour in the area. And of course, that she works for the Schober company. That's why forensics is involved. What do you know, Loretta?"

"It looks like Evelyne Kaltenbrunner and Alexander Schober were a couple. Last Tuesday I saw Mrs. Kaltenbrunner at Schober AG and then again in the evening near Ascona, at a gas station. I spoke to her very directly and didn't beat around the bush. I asked her specifically whether the affair was true and whether she wanted to meet him now. I didn't want her to get away from me again."

"So, how did she react?"

"She was pretty upset. Hesitated at first, but then admitted it. And even mentioned something about a future together that he had promised her. But Alexander Schober hasn't contacted her since he disappeared."

"Strange." Renzo made a few notes and signaled to the waiter for two more espressos.

"Mia cara Loretta. Now a few questions arise."

"Renzo, I assume there is much more to it. Maybe she also knew something that wasn't working properly at Schober AG. There is a laboratory report that disappeared with Alexander Schober."

"What kind of lab report?"

"Apparently there are several irregularities in the numbers. The margin has changed positively for Schober AG, which is actually nothing negative. Just why is still unclear. Purchases may have been made more cheaply, but perhaps to the detriment of quality. That's why Schober commissioned a laboratory test of the meat and sauces. If Schober saw this confirmed, then Burmann would certainly not be happy. Especially since Schober had suggested that he renegotiate the existing shareholding arrangements. After all, Schober developed the innovations for this Wings to Heaven franchise system."

"You mean Schober got in Burmann's way?"

"I don't know, it could be. The lab report should come today. Perhaps Burmann wanted to divert attention with his assignment. He didn't seem so incredibly worried yesterday."

"But this Evelyne Kaltenbrunner. What's she got to do with it? Wait a minute..." His phone buzzed. He stood up and turned towards the lake side that was visible from the café. The few walkers on the lake promenade enjoyed the wonderful view of the mountains and Lake Maggiore.

"Wonderful," thought Loretta, "if only the circumstances were different." Renzo Capuzzi sat down again in his chair.

"We now know more about the body. There are no signs of violence before the fall. The only thing that is striking is that an antidepressant was detected in her body."

"I told you that she seemed upset, but also unassessable. You couldn't tell if she was desperate or aggressive. Burmann had told me that she was on medication and was getting by just fine with tablets.

Her violent nature seemed to be good for his purposes. She was probably very successful as a buyer."

"My goodness," Loretta sighed, "and I wanted to drive her to a hotel on Tuesday evening. But she didn't want to. She was very vehement."

"Perhaps she had something completely different in mind," Renzo remarked.

"Perhaps she knew more about the lab test than she told me. She was also in a relationship with Burmann."

"What, I think with the Schober?"

"Bonta mia! You're like Lars! Women can certainly have several affairs - even at the same time. Women can also have an affair because they want to get information."

"You speak in riddles, Loretta. What exactly do you mean?"

"Sorry, Renzo, but perhaps Evelyne Kaltenbrunner had a plan with Burmann. As I said, she works in purchasing at Schober AG. If that's the case, then what happened to Alexander Schober? I need to know what's in this report and then check Burmann again."

"But what was Evelyne Kaltenbrunner doing in this remote gorge? Did she want to go to Schober?"

"I have no idea, Renzo. Somehow this doesn't make sense yet. But I'll shed some light on it. I have to go, Renzo."

"We'll examine the area around the scene of the accident for possible clues." Renzo walked Loretta to her car, kissed her on both cheeks and was almost tempted to kiss her on the mouth when Loretta swung around and got into the car.

It had to be spring, she thought. It seemed to her that couples in love were strolling everywhere. With Renzo's bitter, forest-smelling perfume still in her nose, Loretta rushed away. She was happy to have to concentrate on the road. The Via S. Gottardo and Cantonale, which led to the highway, with their shopping and gastronomic temples on either side, demanded her full attention. It felt like half the canton was shopping.

18

Loretta opened the current notes on the Schober case on her laptop. Carmen was a treasure! Yesterday she asked Regula to check with the real estate agency whether Alexander Schober had been invited to the agency's party on April 3rd. Regula, with her special nature, had even received the owner's cell phone number as he was currently in Mallorca. She learned from him that Schober was not only a guest, but also a customer and that the sale of his house in the Maggia Valley was sealed that afternoon. With a customer from the large canton, Swiss slang for Germany. Alexander Schober had also demanded confidentiality regarding the sale of the house.

"That was definitely a new development in the case. Why did Alexander Schober sell the house? Why doesn't his wife seem to know about this? Why does no one else seem to? What was he up to and who didn't like it? Was the report perhaps the famous straw that broke the camel's back?"

Loretta stared thoughtfully at her Brenda Superwoman portrait on the wall, which Freddy Mouse had drawn in comic style for her 40th birthday.

Then she dialed Bernadette Schober's cell phone number. Nothing. She could not be reached either by phone or landline. Loretta decided to call Elsie. Did she save her number? Elsie was busy unloading the market stall on the farm at home and reported, quite out of breath, that Bernadette wanted to go to Ticino again. That was two days ago. On Tuesday afternoon she took the train to Ticino. But she didn't want to spend the night in the house, but in Locarno. Elsie was worried, not only for Alexander, but also for her sister. While Loretta was still on the phone with Elsie, a WhatsApp message flashed. It was from Renzo.

"We found Evelyne Kaltenbrunner's car. As soon as I have the test results, I will contact you. Enjoy the evening – even without me, mia cara, Renzo"

"Here comes the latest information on the Schober case," Carmen stood in the doorway and held up a document.

"Come in, Carmen. Is that the lab report?"

"Yes, Regula printed it out straight away." She placed the report on Loretta's closed laptop, as there was no other space on the desk.

"Regula is simply fantastic that she managed to do this so quickly." Carmen nodded and sat down opposite

Loretta. Loretta picked up the printout and began to read.

"I don't think you'll be eating at Wings to Heaven again any time soon! The chicken meat is contaminated with antibiotic-resistant germs that are even resistant to reserve antibiotics. In other words, antibiotics that you use when conventional ones no longer help. There are also indications of a nutritional deficiency; the wings show osteoporosis. My goodness, this is a medical record, not a lab report." Loretta scanned the lines.

"If Alexander Schober has read this, then he must be devastated. He, who trimmed everything towards sustainability and saw new perspectives for Schober AG. If this becomes public, the damage to the company's image will be unparalleled."

Carmen tried to suppress her disgust. "But who knew he had commissioned this analysis?"

"That is the question, my love. If Daniel Burmann knew about it, perhaps through Evelyne Kaltenbrunner as an informant, then Schober was definitely a disruptive factor.

"But why is Evelyne Kaltenbrunner dead now? That doesn't make any sense." Loretta got up, walked around the desk and stopped close to Carmen.

"Maybe Evelyne Kaltenbrunner didn't know anything and only found out about these disgusting things through Alexander Schober. And Burmann bumped off both of them!"

"Carmen, oh God, what a bad influence we have on your beautiful Grisons dialect. Bumped off! But essentially it can't be ruled out." Loretta absentmindedly stroked her hand over the back of her desk chair and sat down again.

"We know that Alexander Schober sold his house in Ticino. Apparently he wanted to keep it to himself. Hmm, does he really want to burn bridges and start a new life with Evelyne Kaltenbrunner? At least that hasn't come true now."

"Maybe he's had enough of everyone" Carmen said. "I could understand, if he wanted to leave to start a new life. His environment is not necessarily friendly. And as a researcher, he is always looking for new challenges that no one has ever dared to tackle before." Carmen hummed the theme song from Star Trek.

"You are a real man-understander! That's certainly not impossible. But would he really leave his family and his wife without a word? With his lover or without?" Carmen shrugged her shoulders and followed up meaningfully: "What do we already know about men in midlife crises?!"

"My dear Carmen, at the age of 64 Alexander Schober should at least be out of this crisis by now. But please try to reach Bernadette Schober. She is said to be in Ticino. And if you don't have any luck, tell her sister to call me. I'm going to Daniel Burmann now."

19

"Mrs. Lombardi, now you're irritating me. It's terrible what happened to Evelyne. But what do you want from me? You're barging in here ..." Daniel Burmann seemed moved and less controlled than before.

"Mr. Burmann, you should know that the meat you are processing in your new machines is contaminated chicken meat, which has nothing to do with the ethical principles you told me about last time. We have a laboratory report that shows the analytical values of the products. The report was commissioned by Alexander Schober. Burmann had turned pale and slumped in his chair. Loretta continued.

"This also explains the much improved purchasing conditions. It's inferior meat, if you can even call it that. It's high-level fraud. The question arises as to what role Evelyne Kaltenbrunner played in this. Maybe that's why she had to die?"

"I didn't know anything about it! I trusted Evelyne. Even if she was different after our little affair. That was fine with me. Because she was loyal to our company and a tough buyer. At least I thought so."

"But Mr. Burmann, you're not telling me that you haven't asked yourself why the purchasing conditions have improved so much."

"Mrs. Lombardi, if I took care of everything in detail, I could run the store myself and save a lot of personnel costs. Evelyne does… – did good work. She was able to negotiate group advantages that others dream of. We have potential franchisees who are just waiting for us to send them the contract. Evelyne skillfully brought this into play with the suppliers. She also talked about the prospects of new products, and their eyes flickered like they were watching a slot machine. They didn't need to know straight away that not everything counts on Wings to Heaven. But they have seen that there is a big business in it."

"That's probably true, but that was also reflected in the inferior quality. And you didn't know about that?"

"No. I was just thrilled with what Evelyne negotiated for us."

"Why should she be so ... ". The phone rang.

"Tell them I'm busy… They should send an email… What on earth do I have to do with this! Who says that?" Burmann loudly banged the receiver down on the system and then typed away on his cell phone.

"Okay, then the press already knows about the dangerous meat at Wings to Heaven! Did you arrange this?" Burmann stared angrily at Loretta.

"You are my client. I am investigating on your behalf. It is not my job to release information to the public. I'm just trying to find out the whereabouts of Alexander Schober and who is driven by what motivation. Has Mrs. Kaltenbrunner not asked herself how such conditions came about? She is not a beginner and should know that it is hardly possible to get high quality for such low prices. I mean, every why has a wherefore."

"I have no idea. We can't ask her anymore. Dead women tell no tales. All I know is that now I have to find answers for these media nonsense. They're really excited that there's another scandal. Do you think I'm getting myself into something like this on purpose? Now that it's finally starting! I need Alex so we can move on. That's my problem. And I commissioned you to solve it!" Burmann stood up, touched the desk and clattered out without farewell.

20

"Loretta, you didn't answer your cell phone. Renzo Capuzzi called. You spoke a message to his combox. Isn't he that fancy detective from that kidnapping case back then." Regula seemed a little different than usual. More relaxed.

"Yes, that's the Clooney-George-Brad-Pitt mix. I'll get myself a quick coffee and then I'll call back."

The kitchen looked tidy, no more exotic teas and strange health products, just Lars' green tea. Loretta cheered internally. Maybe Regula had made up her mind. Maybe for the detective agency. Loretta wanted to wait until Regula approached her, even though it was very difficult for her. Now it was Renzo's turn. Smiling, she entered his speed dial.

"Thanks for your message, Loretta. I read on social media that there was something wrong with the meat at Wings to Heaven. Not really looking good for the company."

"Yes, that is indeed true. The tricky thing is that Burmann apparently really didn't know the extent of it. It was clear to him that Evelyne Kaltenbrunner had gambled on the purchasing conditions, but not under what conditions. Maybe she wanted to trick him. Out of revenge for leaving her."

"Women are capable of anything."

"Oh Renzo, please don't use such platitudes."

"I know how to tease you, mia cara. But the avenging angel thing isn't unreasonable."

"Perhaps she really wanted to burn all bridges - together with Alexander Schober. After all, she wasn't very mentally stable. But why did she hike in this area? You don't just go for a walk in the Ticino mountains - especially not in this fashionable outfit. Is there anything about the traces in her car?"

"There are various traces. We are in the process of decoding them. Those from Alexander Schober are clear. We were able to compare them with his DNA. But we're still working on the others. Among other things, there is also white long hair ... Loretta? Are you still there?"

"Long white hair, where?"

"In the passenger seat of the SUV. Does that ring a bell?"

"This may be a long shot, but Bernadette Schober has long white hair. And she went to Ticino three days ago and hasn't been reachable since."

21

Elsie didn't feel comfortable walking into
Bernadette and Alexander's house like that. She only
had the key for emergencies and that was like a
premonition. An old town house had always been
Elsie's dream. Like she had seen in movies. In Notting
Hill, for example, when Julia Roberts comes down the
stairs and... she stepped on a magazine, advertising
flyers and an envelope. The mailbox flap in the front
door was open. Probably so that the mail slipped
through more easily. She picked up the mail and
studied the sender of the letter. An address in Ponte
Tresa. The doorbell ringing made her jump.

"Is everything ok? I couldn't find a parking space
and am now standing halfway down the driveway."
Loretta looked at Elsie, who was holding the envelope
in front of her like a shield.

"Let's see if everything is okay, Elsie." The light
tone of command got Elsie going again. They went into
the kitchen and inspected the other rooms on the
ground floor and then moved on to the ones upstairs.
Nothing. No abnormalities. Elsie sat down on a chair in
the kitchen and placed the envelope she had been
carrying with her the whole time on the kitchen table.

Loretta went to the window and tried to check her car in the driveway, in the darkness.

"I could use a cherry schnapps now!" Elsie said.

"I'm in." Although Loretta wasn't enthusiastic about hard liquor, she only felt weak when it came to cherry. She also felt cold. The rooms didn't seem heated. How fitting for Bernadette Schober's cold demeanor, she thought to herself, only to immediately reprimand herself. Behind her, Elsie let the refrigerator door close with a thud and approached Loretta with two glasses of ice-cold cherry.

"Jesus, that feels good." Elsie had emptied the glass in one go. Loretta enjoyed the warmth the cherry instantly created.

"Another one? This is a really good *Baselbieter Kirsch*." Elsie was already at the fridge.

"I want to drive us both back. No, thank you." Loretta put the glass on the kitchen table.

"What's your sister's numerological number?"

"Bernadette is a one. She was always the model child in our house. Always tidied up, did well at school, she also completed her training as a pharmacy assistant perfectly and then wanted to study." Elsie drank the second cherry, with pleasure it seemed, and placed the bottle on the table next to the mail.

"She would have liked to take over our father's pharmacy. But he couldn't imagine a woman owning a business. Phew..." She bent her head back to get the last bit out of the glass.

"So our younger brother had to go and study, even though he didn't want to. But who gets what he wants?" It wasn't clear whether Elsie was referring to her own situation or going through the family constellation.

"And what did your sister do instead?"

"She got married," Elsie giggled and poured herself another cherry.

"My father liked Alexander immediately. He met him at a trade fair. Alex was still very young and had only recently joined the family business. He was probably standing completely lost at a Schober trade fair stand when my father spoke to him. My father was actually looking for a machine manufacturer and he found the perfect son-in-law."

Elsie began like a hymn: "Ecco come è iniziata la favola di Bernadette e Alex" and helped herself to the next cherry.

"Was it so magical for your sister too?"

"Bernadette was always obedient and dutiful. I think she submitted and it was good for her. And for me. I had much more freedom. My parents knew that

128

they couldn't decide that much about me. Luigi was a good-for-nothing to them. And then a little younger than me." Elsie briefly crossed herself, kissed the gold cross on her necklace and smiled at Loretta.

"Nevertheless, I made a good choice. We have been married for 30 years now. Bernadette and Alex will be married for 40 years in May. They honeymooned in Ponte Tresa and presto, nine months later Melissa was born."

"Ponte Tresa? What a coincidence. Look at the envelope, Elsie." Elsie held the envelope away from her and squinted to read better.

"May I?" Loretta took the letter and looked at the postmark. Monday, April 7th in Ponte Tresa, Italy but no private address and no name.

"Elsie, do you know of someone, maybe a friend, in Ponte Tresa?"

"No. Bernadette and Alex don't have very many acquaintances. And down there. No. They were in Ponte Tresa on the Swiss side. I know they enjoyed it there. Alex was excited because they went through the Gotthard road tunnel. It wasn't long finished yet. Oh, that was a long time ago," Elsie sighed.

"Elsie, try to reach your sister again."

"Nothing, the combox is on again. I've already spoken up three times. I do not know what's going on. That doesn't suit Bernadette. I'm really worried."

"Elsie, this is an emergency situation, would you please open the letter. Maybe it contains some kind of clue." Elsie fortified herself with another cherry. Then she tore open the envelope.

"The letter is from Alex!"

22

She washed her hands. She couldn't say how often in the last few days. At least very often. The bathroom was small but very clean and practical. Alex would like that, she thought. The cosmetic bag had space on the shelf. But she didn't feel like unpacking. That would be like arriving and that, it wasn't.

Just a short stay and then. She came to this point to wash her hands again and the thought carousel began again. How excited the other woman had been when she had surprised her in the house. She would have been there many times already, waiting for his message. Because everything would be clear, they would leave together. She would have made preparations for that too. Whatever they were. At that moment the doorbell rang. A Mr. Vivace from a clearance company stood there and apologized for just stopping by. But they would start clearing out next week. Whether the plan had already been drawn up as to what exactly was to be disposed of.

Decluttering? In a brief euphoria, she thought it was the start of a new beginning for them both. That he regretted. That he remembered what they had in common here. But then came the disillusionment. She had nothing to worry about, the painting work would not start until the end of April and the handover to the buyer was purely a formality. Everything would already be formally done.

She remembered that she even had to smile and seemed to have a knowing impression. Because Mr. Vivace said goodbye verbosely and said that he would stop by next Saturday, as agreed with her husband, to get the plan. Then one could perhaps briefly discuss whether he should schedule one or two employees for the next week. While she stood there in a daze, this was the sign the other had been waiting for.

Then it clicked. She immediately heard an internal switch being flipped. Something came to light that she recognized from her time in the pharmacy. Distance yourself from what sick people bring to you. Instead, function and lead. It didn't escape her notice that this blonde, angry woman had a problem. She could easily convince her to lead her to the hut where Alexander was supposed to be staying. The stupid woman even saw this as a capitulation on the part of the wife.

So they drove into the valley in her black SUV and up a narrow mountain path. When they couldn't go any further, they got out and kept walking up the steep slope. The other one talked on and on. Then it seemed like a relief, for the other and for herself, when she gave her a strong push at the narrowest part of the path, where they had to walk one behind the other. She was amazed at the power she was able to release. She even remembered - or her hands remembered - feeling a silky material.

23

He looked at the clock nervously. There was a market on the Italian side of Ponte Tresa and the streets were accordingly busy. He had underestimated that. His plan to arrive in Ronchini at 9 a.m. could hardly be kept. The van he had rented was also harder to operate than expected. This was due, on the one hand, to his poor driving skills and, on the other hand, to his excessive fatigue. He had been working on the formulations of the new nutritional supplements for the last few days and nights. He had prepared them so that they were ready for a first test run. He didn't want to waste any more time. He had already registered a company in Italy – just over the Swiss border. He was able to convince a supplier from the old days to produce it. But he needed money. That's why he sold the house. In any case, it was no longer the house it once stood for. He had defiled it. With that thought, he jerked the steering wheel to the left to avoid hitting the car in front of him. He got lucky. Nobody was coming towards him at the moment. He had to find his inner balance again. He briefly stopped his vehicle on the hard shoulder to regroup. Evelyne came back to his mind. She believed in him and actively supported him.

Both in his development work and elsewhere. Bernadette, on the other hand, was slowly getting tired of hearing about his ever-new recipes and of experiencing the disappointments in the company from time to time. Daniel Burmann always focused on speed. Everything had to happen quickly for him.

But then he, Alexander Schober, made his breakthrough. A new sauce concept with which Schober AG became important again with his significant involvement. That was a triumph. And Evelyne at his side, who trusted him even more. Why not create new products from these formulas? Start your own company for both of you! She was interested in him - not just as a partner in Schober AG, but as a man, as a lover. He was intoxicated. He was able to work like never before and still have time for his young lover, who demanded no less of him.

But at some point it just became too much. This back and forth, to Ticino, then 10-hour days in the laboratory, then back home to sleep and change shirts. What had he done? What had he done to Bernadette? After 40 years, her husband would run away with a woman younger than his own daughter.

And then the disaster with the meat. What did Evelyne know? How she suddenly found him in the café in Ascona. Yes, she admitted to purchasing this cheap meat. Intentionally, because she couldn't stand how Daniel Burmann treated her and him. His unbelievable misstep suddenly became crystal clear to him.

"If he didn't stand by her, they would all regret it - all of them!" Those were Evelynes last words. How she spoke, and how she presented herself. Aggressive, like he had never experienced her before. She actually threatened him. He was relieved when she left again. But also worried. What would follow? He had already made it clear to her days ago that their only bond was friendship. Nothing more. She had to realize that there was no future for both of them. He rubbed his eyes and took a sip of water. Another twenty kilometers and then he was finally there. Maybe he could lie down for another hour before packing up his personal belongings in the house and putting them in the car. He had to be fresh at lunchtime.

24

He wanted to turn the key, but the front door wasn't locked.

"Bernadette! You're here already?" He approached her carefully. She stood close to the porch door and looked at him as if she had been expecting him.

"So you got my letter? I am so sorry! Bernadette, I just lost my way. I was no longer myself. I wanted to prove to myself again that I could save the company. That I can keep the family tradition going." He froze and leaned on the chair. Bernadette also stood frozen and looked away.

"Say something, Bernadette. I know I hurt you. I made a fool of myself, but it was basically for you, for you and the children." He sank weakly into the armchair. Bernadette Schober looked at him with such coldness that he shuddered.

"Have you ever, in forty years, not only thought about yourself and the company? You divided the days. You determined the rhythms. You have reduced me to being a spectator of your life, of your defeats and highs." She remained completely calm and continued speaking.

"Or no, I was allowed to help you in the difficult times. I was a participant in your life for a while. Like our children. They were allowed to participate in your life. You abused them emotionally, like you abused me." She looked at him.

"I don't know what to say. I'm so tired. I know I've made mistakes. But I will make up for everything. I have been working on our future these past few days. Believe me, I..."

"You worked on our future? Did you tell your bitch that too? Is that why you sold our house?"

"I wrote to you. I would like to discuss this with you in peace." He began to breathe heavily.

"Bernadette, please let me rest for a moment. I've been working day and night and can't concentrate anymore. I'm not feeling well. My heart. I have a heartache." He clutched his chest.

"Bernadette, please!"

The doorbell rang. Bernadette Schober did not respond. She walked over to the kitchen and poured a glass of water, adding a few drops from an eyedropper. Without a word she went back into the living room and handed the glass to her husband.

"Stop!" Loretta, who had suddenly appeared in the hallway, screamed at the top of her lungs. Beside her,

Beat Hagmann, visibly excited, held the front door key in his hand. Loretta ran towards Alexander Schober. The glass slipped out of his hand in shock. It shattered into thousands of splinters on the stone floor - just like his entire life.

25

"Grüezi everyone," Morita Miramoto came into the tea kitchen beaming with joy. Lars and Loretta paused in their conversation.

"Where are Regula's teas? That orange one with all the threads in it? Creepy." Morita kept his grin, but shook himself slightly.

"Don't touch it. We'll just leave this topic aside," Loretta turned to Morita, who took his cup of green tea and meandered past Lars out of the kitchen.

"Yes, it is a real tragedy. Bernadette Schober almost became a double murderer. First Evelyne Kaltenbrunner and then her own husband."

"How was she going to kill him?"

"Poison. With *Digitalis purpurea*, also called red foxglove. It grows normally in her garden, behind the house. Actually, a heart strengthening agent. But not in higher doses."

"Oh man. I know why I only like green teas and not these herbal blends. But why did it only almost work?"

"I arrived just in time and rushed towards Schober. Freddy Mouse would have been delighted to see me attack him as Brenda Power-Woman. But honestly, it was more of a request that I yelled at Schober not to drink any of the stuff. Because in that moment, everything came together. Bernadette Schober was already suspected of having murdered Evelyne Kaltenbrunner. Then she was in the house, although she couldn't have known anything about the letter from her husband asking her to be in Ronchini on Saturday lunchtime. The pale Alexander Schober in the armchair and no one had answered my bell."

"And then you called *Freeze* and everyone froze," said Morita, who underlined his remark in an Asian fighting stance and joined Loretta and Lars in the kitchen again.

"Nearly. It was more like *Stop* or something like that! At least very loud. Poor Beat Hagmann, he was almost scared to death. And he was so full of compassion for Mrs. Schober."

"My goodness, what a drama. I always ask myself how do you get to such a point when love turns into hate and retaliation," Lars looked at Loretta questioningly.

"Bernadette Schober felt cheated out of her life. But it's hard to say exactly when everything changed. With Evelyne Kaltenbrunner it was achieved fairly quickly. She took Alexander Schober's side and then started a relationship with him. She tried everything to harm Daniel Burmann. To make him jealous. However, for Burmann it had no meaning at all. So she looked for another chance."

"Relationships," Lars grumbled, putting down his teacup.

"And then she took revenge with the cheap meat?"

"Yes, exactly. And she anonymously sent emails with details to all relevant media, like in a crime thriller. Of course, this immediately caused enormous waves. They closed the two companies in Zurich and Basel because activists demonstrated in front of them and drew attention to the conditions at the supplier.

"To be honest, I think that's right. I can't even imagine that I would have eaten that next week. There I am... No, I would have had an appointment at Wings to Heaven in Zurich," said Carmen, who had joined the team and seemed visibly disgusted.

"A tough nut to crack for our client Daniel Burmann. The relationship with the Wings to Heaven franchisor is likely to change significantly, if it remains at all. I think he should have looked at the sources of supply. After all, he was quite successful at imitating the sauces."

"I'm kind of sorry about that. Such a great concept. My favorite food is bumped off, just like that" complained Carmen.

"Carmen has a new favorite expression: *bumped off*", Loretta said laughing, "it's suitable for all occasions."

"True! That's fitting, because it means you've provided a terrible service."

"And what was our missing Alexander Schober up to?" Lars intervened.

"He had everything planned out. A new company in Italy near the Swiss border where he wanted to produce his new nutritional supplements. He has already had prototypes produced there and registration for Europe underway. Actually everything very exciting. He wanted to sell his sauce recipes and his shares to Schober AG. And then dare to start again – together with his wife. He wanted to tell her that in Ronchini. That's why he had asked her there on Saturday. Adding that he was planning something with her in Ponte Tresa. He wanted to tell her that in person. Not only is his new company headquarters located in Ponte Tresa, it is also the place where they spent their honeymoon. This was supposed to be his 40th wedding anniversary gift. Now he'll probably try to save the company from the worst."

"How terrible." Regula stood in the doorway and was visibly moved.

"I always say, *talk to de Lüt*!" All eyes turned to Regula. Nobody dared to say anything.

"Well, if they had all been more open from the start and said what they didn't like, there wouldn't be this tragedy." Everyone nodded - even Lars, who liked to keep his thoughts and statements to himself at first.

"Yes, and that's exactly why I want to tell you that I need a big coffee right now. Tea time is over! Can I now write the final invoice for the customer Wings to heaven while there is still money?"

"With pleasure, Regula. And then we'll all meet for lunch in our restaurant next door! I would say this time it's not chicken crispy, but maybe tarte flambée."

About the authors

Veronika Bellone left her native hometown Berlin shortly after graduating in economics and has lived in Switzerland ever since. Franchising has shaped her live. She has worked as a franchise manager, teaches franchising at universities, advises customers with her own franchise consultancy in Zug and writes specialist and non-fiction books about franchising, among other things.

Thomas Matla was born in Berlin. He studied social and business communication at the Berlin University of the Arts and graduated with a diploma. He has worked for advertising agencies in Berlin, Düsseldorf, Frankfurt am Main, Hamburg and Munich before moving to Switzerland to support Veronika's franchise consultancy in Zug. Together with Veronika he has published several specialist and non-fiction books.

The Disappearance Of Alexander Schober is the first crime novel by the author duo Bellone/Matla, which also marks the start of their new crime series *The Swiss Franchise Detectives*.

German edition

If you are interested in the original German version, don't miss Volume 1 of DIE FRANCHISE-FAMILIE.

DIE FRANCHISE-FAMILIE. **Erster und zweiter Fall der Schweizer Franchise-Detektive Loretta Lombardi und Lars Van de Velde**. Kriminalroman, Band 1 (Doppelband), 302 Seiten, als Paperback & E-Bock erhältlich. Autorenduo: Veronika Bellone & Thomas Matla. Herstellung und Verlag: BoD Books on Demand, Norderstedt (D)

ISBN: 9 783 758 329 883 (Paperback)
ISBN: 9 783 756 285 662 (E-Book)

Erhältlich in den BoD Online-Buchshops:
https://buchshop.bod.de (Deutschland)
https://buchshop.bod.ch (Schweiz)

Veronika Bellone
Thomas Matla

Kriminalroman
Erster und zweiter Fall

DIE
FRANCHISE-
FAMILIE

Epilogue

All cases, events, companies and people depicted as well as the names associated with them are fictional. Any similarities to people, living or deceased, as well as to companies or events, especially within the franchise economy, are purely coincidental and not intentional.

Preview

In the second volume of the Franchise crime series *THE SWISS FRANCHISE DETECTIVES*, Lars Van de Velde is called to the Zug headquarters of the *Happy People* fitness franchise. It relies heavily on *robotics* and *artificial intelligence*, but is being blackmailed. Obviously, not all franchisees act in accordance with the system. During his investigations in Berlin and Hamburg (Germany), as well as Unterägeri and Zug (Switzerland) Lars has to experience first-hand how robots can help, but also endanger human lives.

Licensing

If you as a publisher are interested in a license of this book or others of the author duo for a country or a national language, please contact us without obligation. We would be happy to provide you with further information.

We are the official partner for Bellone/Matla author rights licensing.

Bellone Franchise Consulting GmbH
Poststrasse 24, CH-6302 Zug
Phone 0041. 41. 712 22 11
E-Mail office@bellone-franchise.com
Homepage www.bellone-franchise.com